GOLD FOR BRADY

Sam Brady had no authority as a lawman in California, but this didn't hinder him as he set out to find who was trying to drive Harry Bird off his claim. After meeting the cantankerous old miner, Sam was tempted to leave him to fight his own battles, but the decision was made for him and he soon found that he needed all his skills as a Texas Ranger to survive the ruthless tactics being employed by the claim jumpers ... or was he in greater danger from the attentions of a young woman called Margaret Martin?

GOLD FOR BRADY

GOLD FOR BRADY

by

Wayne Gamble

Dales Large Print Books
Long Preston, North Yorkshire,
BD23 4ND, England.

British Library Cataloguing in Publication Data.

Gamble, Wayne
    Gold for Brady.

    A catalogue record of this book is
    available from the British Library

    ISBN   1-84262-336-2 pbk

First published in Great Britain 1996 by Robert Hale Limited

Copyright © Wayne Gamble 1996

Cover illustration © Lopez by arrangement with
Norma Editorial S.A.

The right of Wayne Gamble to be identified as the author of this
work has been asserted by him in accordance with the
Copyright, Designs and Patents Act, 1988

Published in Large Print 2004 by arrangement with
Robert Hale Limited

Dales Large Print is an imprint of Library Magna Books Ltd.

Printed and bound in Great Britain by
T.J. (International) Ltd., Cornwall, PL28 8RW

ONE

Sam Brady pulled his horse to a halt and listened to the sound of the rifle-fire as it echoed around the hills. It was a number of shots fired from a single rifle, but the echoes made it sound more like a fusillade from many rifles. It had come from further up the valley in the direction that Sam was now headed, and he realized that he would have to be extra careful until he could find its source.

It was mid-afternoon and the sun was already well into its descent as Sam pushed his mount forward once again to follow the well-worn wagon tracks that led along beside the small stream that flowed along the valley floor. Up ahead, he could see where the two hill lines came together to create a deep, steep-sided canyon, out of which this stream flowed. Near the mouth of the canyon he could also see a large pile of rock and gravel, overburden taken from a nearby mine – and it was to this mine that Sam was now heading.

At the mouth of the canyon Sam once again pulled his mount to a halt, only this time it was to survey the mine workings that he could see nestled back against the base of the canyon's eastern wall. The setting was dark and gloomy, the afternoon sun already blocked out by the near vertical rockwall on the western side of the canyon, and the air was noticeably chilly. The stream had been dammed to create a small lake further back up in the canyon, and there was a wooden flume that carried this water over to a small stamp mill that was positioned near the mine entrance. A wooden cabin was built some sixty feet from the mine entrance, and the wagon tracks that Sam had been following led straight past this cabin to the tunnel.

Sam studied the surrounding canyon walls carefully, but there was no sign of the source of the earlier rifle-fire. An uneasiness deep inside him warned him not to trust the tranquil scene offered by the now peaceful canyon, and his hand dropped for reassurance to the low-slung sixgun that was strapped to his right thigh.

'There's nothing to be gained by sitting here all day,' he muttered to himself as he started his horse forward again. Following the wagon tracks, he quickly closed in on the miner's cabin. It was made of rough hand-sawn timber, and the two windows that fronted the stream had heavy wooden shutters secured across them – both of which had shooting apertures cut into them.

On seeing this, Sam pulled his mount to a halt and sat looking at the cabin. He could sense that there was someone inside watching him, so he slid to the ground and tied his horse to a nearby bush before continuing on foot. Movement at one of the windows caused him to stop dead in his tracks, and he tensed on seeing the barrel of a shot-gun being pushed out through one of the shooting holes. He made ready to dive for the cover of a nearby boulder, but stopped when a voice called out to him, 'You get your arse out of my valley before I blow it clean off,' the voice advised. 'I know you come down here to finish me off, but you ain't got me yet, you murdering coyote.'

Sam raised his hand clear of his weapon before replying. 'I'm not looking for any trouble, mister. I've only come here to speak to Harry Bird – and not to cause trouble.'

'I'm not warning you again,' the voice warned. 'If you don't get back on that horse and haul your arse out of my valley I'll shoot you dead.'

'I want to see Harry Bird before...' But Sam got no further before hearing the boom of the shot-gun being fired from inside the cabin. Almost instantaneously he felt the impact of the shot on his body, but he didn't have time to worry about the extent of his injuries as he threw himself to the ground and rolled across the dirt until he reached the cover of a boulder. He lay there not daring to think what damage had been done to his body by the shot-gun blast, but the burning pain in his chest where the bulk of blast had caught him finally forced him to act. Gingerly he unbuttoned his tattered shirt-front expecting to find a nasty open wound, but to his surprise he found only a large red welt.

'What the hell?' he puzzled, as he fingered the area on his chest, but instantly regretted it when the pain turned to a stinging sensation. He let out an involuntary groan as the pain gnawed at his skin, and he was forced to wait with teeth clenched until the stinging had eased some. As the pain subsided his anger increased, and he was sorely tempted to pull his sixgun from its holster and storm the cabin to make the idiot who had fired on him pay dearly for the pain, but he stifled this urge and instead carefully rebuttoned his shirt.

'You in the cabin,' he shouted angrily. 'What the hell do you think you're up to? All I asked was to speak to Harry Bird – and to give him a message from Mike Hall.'

'What was that name again?' the voice demanded from inside the cabin.

Sam made sure he remained well down out of sight behind the rock while he answered this question. 'Mike Hall.'

'Stand clear of that rock and give me a good look at you,' the voice instructed.

'So you can get another shot at me?' Sam scoffed. 'You must think I'm a damned idiot or something.'

'Don't be a cry-baby. I only peppered you with rock-salt, and if you're telling me the truth about Mike Hall you've got nothing to worry about.'

The stinging pain in Sam's chest told him that the voice was telling the truth about the salt. If it had been lead shot he would have been dead by now, or well on his way to bleeding to death, so reluctantly he climbed to his feet and stepped clear of his cover. He could no longer see the shot-gun but movement showed him that there was someone watching him closely.

'Move in closer so I can get a better look at you,' the voice instructed testily.

Sam did as he was bid and walked towards the cabin. He got within fifteen feet of the window before the voice called him to stop.

'What's this message from Mike Hall?'

'I'm not telling you until you put that shot-gun down and come out here,' Sam declared stubbornly.

'I've got a better idea,' the voice offered. 'You come in here, but keep your hand well clear of that sixgun.'

On considering this request, Sam realized that the man was showing trust in him by allowing him to keep his side-arm, so he decided to return this trust and reluctantly moved across to enter the cabin.

TWO

The two shots fired from a sixgun inside the cabin echoed around the canyon walls. The next moment a man, carrying a set of saddle-bags, burst from the cabin and hurried across to mount the horse tied to a bush a short distance away. The rider took one last look back before turning his mount and riding at speed back the way he had come not ten minutes earlier.

The gunman hiding in the rocks high above the cabin watched the horseman disappear through the mouth of the canyon, and realized that by robbing the old miner, this man had very likely done him the favour of killing him in the process. This now only left him with the task of climbing down to confirm that the old man was dead, and to then go and collect the money for a job that unwittingly someone else had done for him.

Sam Brady edged back through the trees. He was nearing the entrance to the canyon once again, only this time he was on foot. He moved across to the base of the rock-wall on the eastern side of the canyon and took cover in some bushes. From this position he could see the eastern wall of the canyon behind the cabin, but was also shielded from view.

The earlier conversation that Sam had had with Harry Bird had been brief and to the point. He had told him that he was in fact a Texas Ranger sent to California by Mike Hall, Harry's brother-in-law, to help him out with the troubles he was supposedly having with some claim jumpers. Harry Bird had quickly apologized for having shot him, but this didn't stop Sam from telling the old miner exactly what he thought of people who shot first and asked questions later. Harry had taken this criticism without complaint – the only defence he offered was that he himself had only just survived being shot at not five minutes before Sam's arrival, by a sniper hiding up on the canyon wall above the mine. This sniper had fired down on him when he was returning to the cabin from the mine – and although several of the bullets had come close, luckily none had hit him.

Believing that the sniper was still up there watching the cabin, Harry had suggested that they go out to see if they could flush him out, but Sam had quickly disagreed with this plan. Instead he put forward his own plan, one that would hopefully fool the sniper into coming to them. After quickly outlining his plan to the old miner, Sam had grabbed up a set of old saddle-bags and stuffed them with some rocks so they looked full and heavy. He had then fired two shots into the cabin floor before running from the cabin and riding at speed from the canyon. On reaching the cover of the trees on the valley floor he tied off his horse and, with rifle in hand, made his way back to the entrance of the canyon to take up position.

It was a full ten minutes before Sam finally saw the gunman picking his way down the steep track on the eastern rock-wall towards the canyon floor. The man stopped every so often to survey the mine diggings below, but he seemed to be satisfied with what he saw and continued on until he finally stepped out on to the canyon floor.

Sam waited until the gunman was walking away from him towards the cabin before he broke cover and moved in behind him. He managed to make it to within twenty feet of him before giving himself away by noisily dislodging a rock with his foot. The gunman turned, but on seeing that Sam had him

15

covered with his sixgun he quickly raised his hands in the air, his rifle still grasped firmly in his right fist.

'Drop the rifle,' Sam instructed, but the gunman ignored this direction and watched through narrowed eyes as the young Texas Ranger closed in on him. The ground that Sam was crossing was a mixture of coarse riverbed gravel and stones, and when inadvertently he stumbled on one of these stones the gunman took the opportunity to swing his rifle down and fire – but the bullet missed its target. Before he could fire again, Sam fired a single shot from his own handgun – the bullet hitting the luckless gunman in the chest and killing him instantly. The gunman fell lifeless to the ground and his rifle flew from his grasp to clatter noisily across the stones.

Sam took a deep breath and waited for his jangled nerves to settle before checking the gunman for signs of life – but he found none. Movement from the direction of the cabin caught his eye, and he looked up to see Harry Bird hobbling towards him.

'You damn near got your head blown off,' the old miner stated matter-of-factly.

'Do you always state the obvious?' Sam asked, with an equal coolness in his voice.

There was no reply to this from the miner and Sam eyed him critically. Harry Bird would be close to sixty years of age, but his bow legs and weathered skin made him look closer to seventy. He had written to his sister telling her of the troubles he'd been having with some claim jumpers, and although he hadn't actually asked for help, the fact that his sister was married to a captain in the Texas Rangers revealed that he must have expected some kind of help to be sent. That help was in the form of Sam Brady, a young ranger who was quick with a sixgun, and had a mind to match. At twenty-two years of age, Sam already had a reputation as a lawman who could make the best of any situation – but on this assignment he had the added obstacle of having no authority in the state of California.

'You know this hombre?' Sam asked the older man.

Harry Bird moved across and looked down at the face of the dead man. 'Yeah – he works for Igor Vlahov.'

Sam waited for Harry to elaborate, but when he didn't, he prompted him, 'Who is Igor Vlahov?'

'He owns the Golden Spirit Mine located on the other side of this hill,' Harry explained, pointing to the eastern wall of the canyon. 'I always knew it was that Russian bandit who was trying to force me off my claim – and now this proves it.'

'Let's not jump to conclusions,' Sam advised him. 'Why don't you just give me the facts and then let me form my own conclusions?'

Harry Bird wasn't too sure how he felt about this curt young man that his brother-in-law had sent to help him. The youngster had long blond hair that hung down to his shoulders, and soft brown eyes that would send any woman's heart aflutter – but how useful he would be in solving his present troubles was yet to be seen. Harry knew Mike Hall wouldn't have sent him someone who wouldn't be able to handle himself if it came to trouble, but the only thing that looked the part about this young man was the cut-away holstered sixgun strapped to his right thigh.

'What exactly do you want to know about Vlahov?' the old miner mumbled peevishly.

Sam took a deep breath. He seriously doubted that he would ever be able to make friends with this old man, so he decided not to waste his time trying. 'Just tell me why you think Igor Vlahov is behind this attempted claim jump – and anything else you think I should know about him and his men,' he prompted patiently.

Harry Bird told Sam about the history of the gold mining in the district, and about Igor Vlahov and the Golden Spirit Mine located on the other side of the rocky hills to the east. Originally the gold had been discovered in the river south of the hills, close to the spot where the town of Wilston was now located. A gold rush had followed – plainly evidenced by the many miners' cabins that were built along the banks of the river. Harry and his partner, George Martin, had arrived some six months after the original discovery and couldn't believe their luck when they found that no one had attempted to try to find the source of the gold being panned from the river. The two men had spent several days talking to the local miners, and had gone on to survey the banks of the river and area to the north of the newly built town of Wilston. Their excitement at finding the place where they thought the gold deposit was located was quickly shattered when they found that a miner already had a claim on the area – but he seemed to be ignorant of the possible gold deposit and was concentrating his efforts on mining the alluvial deposits in the creek. They offered to buy the miner out, but he wanted far too much money for his claim so they decided instead to wait until he was ready to sell at a more reasonable price. They continued to explore the area of the river to the north of this site, and the more they explored, the more they were convinced that this was where the source of the gold was located. One day Harry and George were in town when the news filtered through to them that the miner had sold his claim to a stranger who had recently arrived in town. They had ridden out to the mine to find that the news was correct, and that the stranger was Igor Vlahov. The Russian had paid the miner the full amount he had been asking for his claim, which had left Harry and George little choice but to lament their loss. They were forced to turn their attentions elsewhere in search of gold, and they staked a claim in this canyon where they had found traces of gold in the eastern rock face. Igor Vlahov had gone on to mine his side of the hill in a big way, while the two older miners had gone about it on a much smaller scale. Both mines turned out to be paying concerns, but Harry Bird never forgave Vlahov for stealing the claim on the other side of the hill right from under his nose – the claim that Igor Vlahov called the Golden Spirit Mine.

'So what makes you think that Vlahov is the one trying to drive you off your claim?' Sam asked.

''Cause he's been working that mine for some time now but still hasn't found the motherlode,' Harry explained. 'He found plenty of gold in the first two years, but now only finds enough to cover his costs. He's got some fool idea that most of the gold that was found in the river to the south of here actually came from this canyon, and not from his side of the hill at all – so that's why he made the offer to buy me and George out.'

Sam considered this statement and had to concede that it put Igor Vlahov in a bad light, but decided not to form an opinion until he'd met the Russian mine owner himself.

'Describe this Igor Vlahov to me, and anyone else you think I should know about who works for him.'

Harry Bird gave the younger man a full description of the Russian and his men. After finishing this report the old miner added a question, 'Are you going over to arrest Vlahov right now?'

21

'I've got no authority to arrest anyone in California,' Sam explained patiently. 'I'll take this body into town tomorrow and have a good long talk with the sheriff while I'm there – but right now though I think we should take this body over to the cabin, and then I'll go see if I can find his horse.'

'You'll find it somewhere up there,' Harry Bird declared sullenly, and pointed to the narrow trail that the gunman had earlier descended. 'But don't expect me to help you – because I'm no mountain goat.'

Sam was tempted to respond to this comment, but instead grabbed the dead gunman by the arms and lifted him up on to his shoulders.

'Bring the rifle with you,' he instructed, before moving off towards the cabin.

Harry Bird did as he was bid, and followed along behind the young Texas Ranger.

THREE

Leaving the gunman's body with Harry Bird, Sam retrieved his own horse from just beyond the mouth of the canyon, and he returned it to the cabin before setting off in search of the dead man's mount. Climbing the steep track that led up the canyon wall he soon found the place where the gunman had been firing down on the cabin below. The surrounding area was strewn with empty rifle shells, and Sam guessed that this wasn't the first time the gunman had used this spot to fire down on Harry Bird and the camp below.

Sam then moved on towards the top of the hill and found the gunman's horse tethered in behind a boulder. The horse was still saddled, and seemed quite at ease when the young Texas Ranger climbed up on to its back and started it along the well-marked trail that led towards the west. He had soon covered the 400 yards across the top of the hill to where the ground began to drop away into the valley on the other side, and then he reined in and sat viewing the scene below him with interest.

This side of the hill was much more gently sloping than the eastern side, and it eased down into a broad valley that had a wide river flowing through it. A pile of over-burden could be seen heaped at the foot of the slope, and a narrow tramline built on wooden trestles was used to carry this waste from the mine shaft to its dumping area. Judging by the size of the stamp mill, and the number of well-constructed buildings, Sam surmised that this was a large oper-ation. From where he was sitting he couldn't see the entrance to the mine itself because it had been cut back into the face of the hill below him, but he could see some of the workers moving around near the stamp mill. He sat there watching these men for some time before finally deciding to ride down into the mining camp to confront Igor Vlahov with the news of his dead employee.

Sam followed the trail as it angled down the face of the hillside towards the south until it finally flattened out on to the valley floor and met up with a more established road. He then turned the horse north along this road and headed for the Golden Spirit Mine. When he was a short distance from the mine, Sam guided his horse over to the side of the road and sat surveying the distant workings. There were three men working at the entrance to the mine, and five more manning the large stamp mill. Two of these men walked away from the stamp mill towards the main buildings – and when one of them spotted Sam sitting at the roadside he pointed him out to his companion. Both men stopped walking and stood watching Sam, forcing him to start his mount forward once again towards the mine. He followed the road as it crossed over the canal that was used to return the water from the stamp mill to the river, and then swung over to where the two men were standing waiting.

'What can I do for you, stranger?' the shorter of the two men asked, as Sam pulled his mount to a halt in front of them. 'And what are you doing on Steve's horse?'

Sam eyed the two men with interest. The shorter of the two matched the description that Harry Bird had given of Igor Vlahov, but strangely he spoke in clear and precise English and not with a heavy Russian accent as Sam would have expected. He was of average build and aged somewhere in his mid-fifties, and his body was trim and muscular. He sported an impressive handle-bar moustache, and showed off several gold teeth when he spoke. The second man could be no one else but Jim Carlton – the foreman at the Golden Spirit Mine. He stood around six feet five inches tall with broad muscular shoulders, but it was obvious that the many pints of beer that he had consumed over the years had left their mark on his waistline. Carlton was aged somewhere in his mid-thirties, and his face was set in a scowl as he eyed Sam in return.

'You were asked what you're doing on Steve Wood's horse, mister,' Carlton snarled threateningly.

'I'm looking for Igor Vlahov,' Sam replied, ignoring the foreman's menacing manner, but resting his right hand on his thigh, close to his holstered sixgun.

'I'm Igor Vlahov,' the shorter man assured him. 'So how about telling me what you're doing on that horse.'

'Steve Wood is dead – I was forced to kill him not half an hour ago,' Sam told him bluntly.

'You murdering coyote,' Carlton snarled, as he stepped forwards and reached for Sam – but he stopped mid-action when he saw that the young Texas Ranger already had his sixgun levelled on him.

'Don't be so foolish as to make the same mistake as your friend Wood,' Sam warned, and relaxed when the big man backed away with his hands in the air. 'I killed Wood because he didn't give me any choice. He was firing down on Harry Bird from the ridge above his cabin, and when I got the drop on him he decided to see how good a shot I am – and now he knows. I'm going in to deliver his body to the sheriff in the morning – and to report my actions to him.'

'Did you say that Steve was firing down on Harry Bird's cabin?' Igor Vlahov enquired.

'Yes, and by what I saw he was determined to make sure that he finished Harry off once and for all.'

'I can't think why Steve would want to do that, but then there was a time I could have killed the old fool myself,' the Russian confessed bitterly. 'He peppered me with that damned shot-gun of his when I went over there to make him an offer for his claim. It took more than a week for the red marks from the rock-salt to finally go away.'

Sam lifted his left hand and touched his shirt. He knew exactly what Igor Vlahov had gone through, but he didn't mention this to the mine owner. 'Harry is a touch quick on the trigger at times,' he offered in the old miner's defence. 'But I guess when your men are doing their best to kill him, he's got good cause.'

Vlahov's face flushed with anger at this comment. 'If you are trying to accuse me of being responsible for Steve Wood's actions you can think again, young man. Steve Wood worked for me as a night-guard, and what he did in his own time during the day was his own business.'

This answer was what Sam had expected, and he sat eyeing the two men standing before him. Jim Carlton was watching him with eyes that clearly told him that if given half a chance he would readily tear Sam apart with his bare hands – and Igor Vlahov's face showed an equally angry expression, but his was more one of indignation.

'I'll be riding into town tomorrow morning with Wood's body,' Sam informed them again. 'If you want to meet me at the sheriff's office, I'm sure the sheriff would be more than pleased to hear from you – and it will probably save him a trip out here.'

Jim Carlton's face turned even redder after this, and Sam thought for a moment that he was going to rush him, but the still levelled sixgun had a sobering effect on the giant man, and Sam decided it was high time he left.

'I wish you gentlemen both a very good afternoon,' he smiled amiably, before then turning his mount and heading back the way he had ridden only minutes earlier. With a final glance back over his shoulder, he reholstered his sixgun and pushed his mount into an easy canter along the road to the point where the stream that flowed through Harry Bird's valley met up with the river. The sun was low in the sky as he turned his horse along the track that led towards Harry Bird's cabin.

FOUR

The rattle of the wagon as it approached along the road from the direction of the town of Wilston could be clearly heard by Sam at a distance, so he guided his horse over to the side of the road and waited for it to pass. While he waited he ran an eye over the ropes that secured the body of the dead gunman across the saddle of the horse he was leading. It was just after six o'clock in the morning and he was on the way into town to deliver the gunman's body to the sheriff.

Sam and Harry had stayed up late the previous evening talking over the events that had prompted the old miner to write to his sister for help. He had told Sam of the two years of hard work that he and his partner, George Martin, had put into developing their mine into a paying concern, and how everything had turned bad since Igor Vlahov had become interested in their mine some six months back. The Russian had ignored the presence of the two older miners on the opposite side of the hill up until this point, but after they had firmly rejected his offers to buy them out they had become the target of terror tactics. George Martin had finally given in to the pressure some six weeks back and had moved into town to live with his widowed sister-in-law, Elizabeth, who in partnership with George owned the local general store. Harry Bird, being more stubborn than his partner, had hung on determinedly and had refused to be driven off his claim.

The last time Harry had seen the Russian was just after his old partner had left for town. Vlahov had arrived at the mine on his own but before he had a chance to speak Harry had let fly at him with his shot-gun. Vlahov had limped away with a skin full of rock-salt shot, and hadn't made a reappearance since.

The wagon was much closer now, and Sam could see that it was carrying two females. The woman holding the reins was in her mid-forties, and she was dressed in a dark-coloured dress with a shawl draped across her shoulders. Her face was stern and un-smiling, and a deep frown creased her brow as she studied Sam and his accompanying pack-horse. Her companion was much younger, and was in her early twenties. She had the same face-shape as the older woman, but her features were much more relaxed and friendly as she smiled across at Sam.

The older woman stopped the wagon beside Sam and spoke out warily, 'Is that Steve Wood's body?'

'I believe so,' Sam answered honestly, and was conscious of the younger woman's eyes watching his every move.

'Is Harry Bird all right?' the older woman continued.

'Yes, he's fine,' Sam assured her. 'But may I have the pleasure of knowing who's asking – and how you know about this being Steve Wood's body?'

'I'm sorry, young man,' the woman apologized. 'I didn't mean to forget my manners but I was worried for Harry's welfare – that's all. My name is Elizabeth Martin, and this is my daughter Margaret. We were on our way out to drop some food off to Harry when we ran into some of Igor Vlahov's men just outside town. They told us about Steve Wood being shot out at Harry's place yesterday.'

Sam considered this answer momentarily before introducing himself to the women. 'My name is Sam Brady – and you would be

George Martin's sister-in-law, if I have guessed correctly?'

'You have guessed correctly, young man – but you must go on and tell us about this shooting.'

Sam went on to relate the events of the previous day to the two women, all the time conscious of the unwavering gaze of Margaret. He began to feel flustered by her unbridled interest in him, and he felt relieved when he finally finished his story and the older woman spoke again.

'Well, I'm glad to hear Harry wasn't hurt, and I wish to thank you for helping him,' she stated warmly.

'It was nothing really,' Brady replied self-consciously.

'You must come and visit us when you are in town, Mr Brady,' the younger woman purred. 'We would be pleased to have you.'

Sam nodded his acceptance. 'I'll do that, Miss Martin – and please call me Sam.'

'And you must call me Margaret,' she replied, and then gave him a mischievous smile that made him feel even more uncomfortable.

This sultry-eyed young woman was making him feel like a shy young kid with her flirtatious looks, and Sam decided that he had to get away from her before she turned him into a complete babbling wreck. 'It's been nice meeting you ladies, but I must get into town now,' he declared. 'And I hope I'll see you both again soon.'

'Yes, we will be looking forward to that, Mr Brady,' the older woman assured him warmly, and she then started the wagon moving along the road once again.

The younger woman twisted on the seat and gave Sam one last smile that served to make his blood pulse even faster through his veins. He was forced to take several deep breaths to steady his heartbeat before he could start his mount along the road once again. He tried to push the girl from his mind and concentrate on what he intended doing once he reached town with the gunman's body, but Margaret Martin kept coming back into his mind. He had just about given in to the pleasure of remembering her pretty face and the unmistakeable message her sultry brown eyes had given him, when something the girl's mother had said jumped back into his mind. She had stated that they had run into some of Igor Vlahov's men just outside town, and Sam wondered why they had been on the road this early in the morning? It might be that they were just going into town to carry out some business, but for them to do so this early in the morning made Sam suspicious. He realized that he would have to be extra careful from here on into town, and that if he was foolish enough to let his concentration wander on to the girl once again he might well end up dead.

The roadway was deeply potholed, and was in dire need of some major repairs, but Sam was too busy keeping a wary eye on the surrounding countryside to notice this. His horse cantered along at an easy pace under him, able to pick its own way around the worst of the potholes without him even noticing it doing so.

Sam was still some two miles from the town when he saw movement in amongst some bushes off to his left. Instinctively, he threw himself sideways just as a noise that sounded like an angry bee buzzed past his ear, followed shortly by the sound of a rifle shot. A second shot closely followed the first, but this also missed its target because Sam was already falling to the ground where he lay motionless. He landed in an awkward heap, but his hand was firmly clasped around the butt of his still holstered sixgun. He had no choice but to stay where he had landed because it was at least fifty feet to the nearest cover, and he knew that it would be suicide to make a run for it. He assumed by the sound of the rifle-fire that there was only a single ambusher in amongst the bushes and he hoped that he would be able to fool him by playing dead, a ploy which caused Sam some misgivings when two more bullets kicked up the dirt only inches from his head. To his relief these were the last shots fired at him and he forced himself to remain motionless in the middle of the road, listening for any noises that might tell him what the ambusher was up to. It wasn't long before Sam heard the sound of gravel crunching under someone's boots, and the ambusher's long shadow, thrown by the early morning sun, moved into sight.

He stopped some ten feet from the young Texas Ranger, his rifle aimed at Sam's prone figure. The sound of Sam's horse snorting nervously drew the man's attention momentarily, and when he turned back he found Sam was already up on one knee with his sixgun levelled on him.

Before Sam could speak he saw the man bringing his rifle to bear on him again, so was forced to fire his own weapon first. The sixgun in his hand barked out twice, and the ambusher fell to the ground, dead.

FIVE

The outskirts of the town of Wilston came into view as Sam rounded the corner in the road. He had passed through the town the previous day when he had been on his way out to find Harry Bird's mine, but now he allowed himself the time to take in the details of the town. Wilston had a permanent population of around fifty people, and was situated on the banks of the Baron River. The town had grown quickly to service the needs of the thousands of miners who had flooded into the area after the discovery of the alluvial gold and now that this gold was close to being mined out the town had become more dependent on the Golden Spirit Mine for its future. There was only a handful of miners left trying to scrape a living from the meagre amounts of gold still found in the sandy-bottomed river, and the dwindling supply was evidenced by the number of abandoned shacks and cabins on the banks of the river. The business centre of the town also had its fair share of abandoned buildings, but the town would continue to live on as long as the Golden Spirit Mine continued to bring money into the area.

The town was quiet as Sam entered the outskirts and rode along the main street towards the business centre. He was now leading two horses with bundles tied across their saddles – the second being the ambusher he had killed on the road into town. A feeling of relief settled over Sam when he spotted the sheriff's office located next door to the saloon. He was keen to be rid of the bodies, and to have a talk with the local lawman about the attempt on his life.

After pulling his horse to a halt outside the front of the law office, Sam dismounted. He was tying the reins of the horses to the hitching rail when the front door of the law office swung open and the sheriff stepped out on to the boardwalk. The lawman then stood and surveyed Sam and the pack-horses with their bundled loads without speaking.

The sheriff of Wilston was in his mid-fifties, and stood around five feet eight inches tall. He was well fleshed on his face and body, and his hair was grey and receding. He had a casual look about him that hinted of apathy, but Sam knew better than to allow this impression to colour his opinion of the lawman.

'Are you Sheriff Tom Mandall?' he asked.

'Sure am – and who might you be?' the lawman demanded.

'Do you mind if we go inside to talk?' Sam requested, noticing that there were two men standing at the front of the saloon showing interest in their exchange.

The lawman answered this request by turning and walking back into the law office, and Sam followed after him. He noted as he moved across towards the office door that the two men at the front of the saloon were now involved in a furtive conversation, but he pushed them from his mind as he entered the law office.

'You were about to tell me who exactly you are?' the lawman prompted from where he stood at the pot-bellied stove pouring coffee into a couple of tin mugs.

'My name is Sam Brady, and I'm a Texa Ranger.'

'You're a long way from your home territory,' the lawman opined as he handed Sam one of the tin mugs. 'What brings you to my town, and who have you got tied across those pack-horses out there?'

Sam sat down on a chair placed back against the wall before recounting the events that had welcomed his arrival at Harry Bird's

41

mine. He also related the conversation he'd had with Igor Vlahov and Jim Carlton at the Golden Spirit Mine the previous day, and the details of the ambush he'd experienced on the road into town.

The lawman listened to the younger man's story without interruption until he had finished. 'You say that Vlahov said this gunman might be Steve Wood? Did you find any sort of identification on the body that would support this theory?'

'No – nothing,' Sam confessed. 'But both Igor Vlahov and Jim Carlton identified his horse straight away – and Harry reckons he's seen him in town with Jim Carlton on several occasions.'

'I know Jim Carlton,' the sheriff mused. 'He's a real mean customer, and I'd want some pretty damning evidence of his involvement in this before I'd consider fronting him about it.'

'Are you afraid of him?' Sam frowned.

'Hell no – but I've got enough sense to make sure that I've got my facts straight before taking on trouble,' the old lawman declared. 'Let's go out and have a good look at this second dead body you've hauled in.'

The two men moved out into the street, but stopped dead in their tracks when they found that both the pack-horses and their bundled loads were missing.

'Who the hell's playing games?' Sam asked angrily, as he moved further into the street and quickly surveyed the area for signs of the horses. After realizing the futility of trying to find the horses' tracks amongst the many tracks that marked the street, Sam turned to find that the two men who had been standing at the front of the saloon on his arrival were also missing – and he pointed this out to Tom Mandall.

'That was Mike and Glen Wooley, and they both work for the Golden Spirit Mining Company,' the sheriff informed Sam. 'But I think we should go and check if they're still in town before we go jumping to conclusions.'

The sheriff walked towards the saloon and Sam followed along behind him. They entered the bar room and stood looking around at the few patrons gathered there. The two men they were seeking were standing at the bar talking to the barman, and the sheriff led the way straight to them. As they drew near, one of the two men looked up into the large mirror behind the bar and saw them approaching. He nudged his brother on the arm to draw his attention to them, before then turning to face them. 'What can I do for you, Sheriff?' he asked.

'Did you happen to see who took those two pack-horses from outside my office, Mike?' the sheriff quizzed the older of the two brothers.

'What pack-horses would that be, Sheriff?' he enquired with a twisted grin on his lips.

Sam's anger rose inside him. 'You know damn well what pack-horses,' he declared. 'You two were showing enough interest in them just before I went inside the sheriff's office so it can't be all that hard to recall.'

'Are you accusing us of something?' the younger of the two brothers demanded as he too turned to face Sam. His hand hovered close to the butt of his low-slung, cut-away holstered sixgun, and he looked ready to use it. Mike Wooley smiled at this aggression shown by his younger brother, but he made no move to intervene.

'You should think twice before you go for that gun,' Sam warned calmly, but he was taking no chances and his hand hung close to the butt of his own sixgun.

'I'm no Steve Wood, mister,' Glen Wooley snarled. 'I want to see just how fast you really are with that slick-looking side-arm of yours.'

'Hold on you two – just cool down,' the sheriff advised them quickly. 'I'd prefer it if you were to stay out of this, Sam – and you calm down, Glen. We only came in here to ask you two if you saw what happened to those two pack-horses – and that's all.'

Sam relaxed his stance, but he continued to watch Glen Wooley's eyes for any sign that might indicate that he was intending to draw his weapon.

'Maybe you're scared of me, mister,' the younger Wooley brother challenged. 'Maybe you back-shot Steve Wood and you're really just a yellow-bellied coward.'

Before Sam could react to this taunt, Mike Wooley stepped forward and positioned himself between his brother and Sam to prevent further hostility. Glen Wooley took this as a directive, and without speaking turned away and faced the bar. The older Wooley brother then went on to answer the sheriff. 'No, we don't know what happened to those two pack-horses, Tom. Straight after you two went inside your office we came in here to get ourselves a drink, and we've been in here ever since. Joe will vouch for us.'

The sheriff turned his attention to the barman, who was standing behind the bar listening to their exchange. He quickly nodded his agreement to Mike Wooley's statement, and the sheriff nodded his acceptance of this and turned to face Sam.

'I think you should come with me so we can have a talk in private,' he directed, and Sam reluctantly did as he was bid.

The two men walked from the bar room and were back out in the street before the sheriff spoke again. 'I don't want any trouble in my town. You may be a Texas Ranger but you don't have any authority here in California. If you get into a gunfight in my town I'll throw you behind bars just as quick as anyone else around here – so be warned.'

'Those two in there are lying through their teeth, Tom,' Sam insisted angrily. 'Harry Bird told me that you'd done very little to catch the men who've been trying to drive him off his claim, and now I can see what he meant.'

This accusation brought anger to the lawman's face, but his voice was cool and measured when he spoke. 'I told you before that I'll only act when I've got hard evidence to go on. Yes, those men were lying in there, but I also know that barman very well – and he was telling the truth. I intend biding my time until I can find out exactly what they did with those pack-horses, and then I'll go speak to them again.'

Sam's anger quickly dissipated and he felt embarrassed by his outburst. Sheriff Tom Mandall was a methodical type of lawman who didn't run off half-cocked – and this was in no way a bad trait. He reminded Sam of Tate Sharp, the old bounty hunter who had taken him under his wing when he was just sixteen years of age. He and Tate had then worked as partners for close on four years until Tate was killed in an ambush that had been set up by a gang of killers they were trailing at the time. After burying his old companion by the trail-side, Sam had set out after the outlaws – but several of them chose to die under his guns rather than face the hangman's noose.

'I'm sorry about the outburst, Tom,' Sam apologized. 'I usually don't run off half-cocked like that.'

'That's OK, son,' the sheriff declared. 'I've been told by more than one person before today that I'm as slow as a mule, and that I can frustrate people at times.'

'What are you planning to do next?'

'I'm going to sniff around to see if I can find anyone who saw what happened to those horses – and I suggest you go and cool your heels somewhere until I get back to you.'

'Why can't I go with you?'

'Because no one is going to talk to me about what they saw with a stranger hanging around,' the sheriff explained bluntly.

Sam gave in to the sense behind this reasoning. 'OK – you'll be able to find me over at the general store with George Martin if you want me.'

He then watched the lawman move off up the street before leading his horse off in the opposite direction.

SIX

The general store was an impressive structure. It was a double-storeyed wooden building that had been built by a craftsman who knew his trade. The building was made to last, and it looked as if money had been no object in its construction. The lower floor was the shop and store-room and the upper floor was where Harry Bird's partner, George Martin, lived with his sister-in-law and niece.

Sam tied his horse off to the hitching rail outside the front of the store and stepped up on to the boardwalk. On entering the store, he stood and surveyed the impressive array of stock displayed in the wall-racks and on trestle tables around the floor. A counter was built the full length of the shop on Sam's right, and a man was standing behind the counter watching him with interest.

'Can I help you, stranger?' the man asked.

'You can if you're George Martin,' Sam replied lightly as he moved towards the counter.

'I might be him,' the man answered warily.

'Why would you be asking?'

'Harry Bird sent me in to talk to you,' Sam stated, but on seeing the look of doubt that registered on the man's face he went on to explain, 'I'm not here to cause you trouble – I'm here to help you.'

The man still eyed Sam warily, and seemed no closer to being at ease even after this assurance. 'What kind of help do you think I would be needing?'

George Martin was a short skeletal figure, with rounded shoulders and a hawk-like face. Martin's small bird-like eyes remained locked on to Sam, and it was impossible for the young Texas Ranger to read what he was thinking from the expression on his face. If the story that Harry Bird had related about the intimidation that he and George Martin had suffered these past few months was correct, Sam could understand the older man being wary.

'My name is Sam Brady, and I'm a Texas Ranger,' Sam told him. 'I've come to help you fight against the men who are trying to drive you and Harry off your claim.'

The little man sighed, and seemed less than impressed by what he had just heard. 'That damned old fool is just going to get us both killed by his pig-headedness. I don't want your help, young man – I just want Harry to agree to sell his half of the mine so I can sell up too.'

'I thought you wanted to keep the mine?' Sam asked him, confused. 'Harry told me you only left the camp because you were afraid of the claim jumpers.'

'That's true, I am afraid of them, but I also got sick and tired of trying to talk Harry into selling the claim so we wouldn't have to worry about them. It's bad enough having to live half your life worrying about being buried alive under thousands of tons of dirt and rock, much less also having to worry whether someone was going to shoot you every time you came up to the surface. We were made a good offer for the mine, and it is only Harry Bird's pig-headedness that is stopping me from becoming a very rich man who'd never have to risk his life again.'

This news stunned Sam. He had come to understand from Harry's story that his partner was as keen as himself to be able to work their claim in peace, but this now put a whole new slant on it. 'Why don't you sell your half of the claim and leave Harry to sort it out with his new partner?' he asked.

'Me and Harry have been partners for well over fifteen years, and we've never let each

51

other down. I'll stay here in town and wait until he's had enough of being shot at – and then we can both retire in peace.'

'That may well happen, but Harry seemed as determined as ever when I spoke to him,' Sam informed him. He then went on to tell him about the gunman he had shot the previous afternoon in the canyon, and finished by admitting that he had lost the man's body not fifteen minutes earlier outside the sheriff's office.

'Before this man died did he happen to tell you who was behind these attacks on me and Harry?' Martin enquired eagerly.

'No, he died instantly,' Sam replied. 'But we have established that his name was Steve Wood, and that he was one of Igor Vlahov's men.'

The sound of footsteps drew the two men's attention, and they turned to see a man enter the store. This man walked across to join them at the counter before speaking. 'Are you the young man who shot Steve Wood?' he asked directly.

'That's correct,' Sam replied as he eyed the man warily. 'And who might you be?'

'My name is James Morgan, and I'm the president of the Local Business Association,' the man answered.

Sam looked across at George Martin and got a nod of the head from the shop owner to support this claim, and then returned his gaze to the president of the Local Business Association. James Morgan was aged in his mid-fifties, and had a large bloated body. The skin on his face was loose and it sagged into jowls at his jawline, and his face was covered with beads of perspiration. He was dressed in a dark, ill-fitting suit that hung off his body like a tent, and his jacket was dirty and food-stained.

'What exactly can I do for you, Mr Morgan?' the young Texas Ranger asked.

'I have been speaking to the sheriff, and he told me you've come here to help out Harry Bird. I was hoping you might be able to help us all out by talking some sense into that old fool – and convincing him to sell out to Igor Vlahov.'

Sam considered this request for a moment. 'What exactly has it got to do with you whether Harry sells out or not, Mr Morgan?'

An indignant expression registered on Morgan's face, and he became flushed in the face as he answered. 'I've a lot of money invested in this town, and I want to make sure it has a future,' he retorted.

'I still don't understand how Harry selling

his claim to Igor Vlahov will help this town?'

James Morgan shook his head patron-izingly. 'It's really simple if you think about it, young man. The future of Wilston relies heavily on the employment generated by the Golden Spirit Mine, and if the mine was to close down because there was a lack of viable gold-bearing ore it would spell the end of the town.'

'He's right, youngster,' George Martin attested. 'Igor Vlahov has claimed that the Golden Spirit Mine is becoming uneconomic to mine, and unless he has access to the ore located in the western side of the hill, he'll be forced to close down within six months.'

'I'm afraid that there is nothing I can do to help you with that problem, Mr Morgan. I'm here to help Harry Bird to protect himself from the people who have been trying to drive him off his claim, and when I find who's behind it they will be facing jail for their crimes. I suggest that if you know any-one who is mixed up in it, you let me know right now.'

James Morgan's face flushed with anger, he looked as if he was about to explode. 'How dare you?' he spluttered. 'I have never been so insulted before in all my life. You dare to accuse me of being part of this just because I have the interests of the town in mind?'

'I never said you were involved in it, I just asked that you tell me if you know anyone who might be involved.'

'It's the same thing to me, young man,' Morgan snarled. 'You could well do with learning some manners when dealing with your betters, and don't bother asking for any help in the future.' Morgan then turned on his heel and stormed out of the store, leaving a stunned Sam and George in his wake.

'I seem to have touched a raw nerve there,' the young Texas Ranger mused.

'You could be right, but I doubt it, Sam,' George Martin reflected. 'James Morgan owns both the grain store and the Golden Nugget Saloon, so he has a lot of money invested in this town, but I don't think he's capable of this sort of violence.'

Further talk was forestalled when Sheriff Tom Mandall entered the store. 'Can I speak to you outside for a moment, Sam?' he asked.

'Yes, I've nearly finished here,' Sam announced before turning back to George Martin. 'I'll have a talk to Harry about what you've told me, and maybe I can convince him to see the sense in your argument – but I can't promise you anything.'

George Martin beamed a smile and

reached out and grasped Sam's hand and shook it warmly. 'Believe me, it is the best thing for him and me both.'

'Remember that I said I can't promise you anything,' Sam said before turning and walking from the store with the local lawman.

Once outside in the street, the sheriff looked around to make sure that no one was within hearing distance before speaking. 'I had another talk with the barman at the saloon, and he told me that Mike and Glen Wooley did come back into the bar room as they claimed, but they spoke to another man sitting at one of the tables, and he got up and left straight afterwards. That man was a prospector named Martin Beller who has a small riverbank claim to the south of town. He's often been seen drinking with the Wooley brothers.'

'That all ties in nicely,' Sam proclaimed. 'So what are you going to do now?'

'The Wooley brothers rode south out of town just after we spoke to them earlier, so I intend riding out to see if I can find them.'

'Do you mind if I tag along?'

'You're welcome, son,' the older lawman smiled. 'But just remember who's running this show.'

'Point taken,' Sam assured him.

SEVEN

The two men stopped their mounts on a ridge that looked down on one of the many miners' cabins that were built along the banks of the Baron River.

'That's Martin Beller's cabin below, and those horses standing out front look like the Wooley brothers' mounts,' the sheriff informed Sam. 'If Beller did take the horses from outside my office, he'd very likely have them stabled in that lean-to at the side of his cabin.'

Sam made no reply to this, and waited for the lawman to go on to outline his plan for their next move. He liked Sheriff Mandall, but he found the lawman's laconic manner frustrating at times, and had to fight the urge to hurry him up.

'We could ride straight down there and call them out, but I feel that would be dangerous,' Mandall mused. 'We would be better served splitting up and covering the house front and rear before calling on them to surrender.'

'I agree with that,' Sam quickly acknow-
ledged. 'And I also think that it would be a
good idea if we could make sure that the
pack-horses are definitely in that lean-to
before we call them out.'

The sheriff nodded his head pensively.
'You've got a good head on those shoulders
for such a young man,' he reflected. 'You
want to take the back of the cabin?'

'Yes, and I'll also check the lean-to if you
want.'

'Let's go,' the older lawman commanded,
and pushed his mount forward towards the
cabin.

The two men closed to within 200 yards of
the cabin before splitting up and heading off
in separate directions. There were plenty of
trees and bushes growing around the cabin
and when both men dismounted, they were
able to make it into position on foot without
being challenged.

Sam was carrying his rifle, but on reaching
his position in the cover of some bushes
located some thirty feet from the rear of the
cabin, he laid the rifle aside and drew his
sixgun. His plan was to move in close to the
rear of the cabin, and he felt that the rifle
would hinder his progress. He stayed in the
cover of the bushes for several more minutes

straining his ears for any sounds that might indicate the presence of the men inside the cabin, but he heard nothing. Finally, he dashed across the open ground towards the cabin, his heart pounding in his chest as he ran. On reaching the wall of the cabin he found he was short of breath, and Sam stood still and waited for his breathing to settle back into an even rhythm. The sound of voices could now be clearly heard, and one of the men inside the cabin laughed loudly. Sam ignored it and moved off towards the door of the lean-to. He lifted the wooden latch and eased the door open. The rusted hinges squeaked faintly and Sam swore silently to himself as he listened to see if the men inside the cabin had heard it. Their voices continued without halt, and Sam edged in through the doorway and stood looking around the interior of the lean-to.

There were three horses inside the ramshackle structure, and Sam instantly recognized two of them as the ones he had left outside Tom Mandall's office that morning. Both horses still had on their saddles – but the bodies of the dead gunmen were no longer strapped across their backs. Sam checked the inside of the lean-to for signs of the bodies – but there was none to be found. He realized that the men would have been stupid to bring the bodies back here, and had probably buried them out in the scrub somewhere where they might never be found again – but they had made a big mistake by bringing back the pack-horses. This was solid evidence that they had taken the bodies from outside the law office, and they would now have to answer to the law for their actions.

He moved back to the door and was about to edge out through the opening when he heard the sound of a hammer being drawn back on a sixgun. He stopped dead in his tracks and saw Glen Wooley standing just outside, his sixgun held at arm's length, and aimed directly at Sam's head.

'Well, what have we here?' Wooley sneered. 'If it isn't the yellow-bellied gunfighter who hides behind an old man with a sheriff's badge to protect himself.'

'I'm here with Sheriff Mandall, Wooley,' Sam warned, as he eyed the gunman warily. 'You can make it easier on yourself by giving me that sixgun, and then telling your brother and Martin Beller to give themselves up too.'

Glen Wooley laughed humourlessly, and then motioned Sam to move out into the open. Then, Wooley lowered his weapon and reholstered it.

'Does this mean that you're giving your-self up?' Sam asked warily.

'It means that you either draw your sixgun, or you die right where you stand,' Wooley growled, and he grabbed for his own gun.

Sam had his gun in his hand and brought it to bear well before his opponent could get his weapon clear of his holster. His gun bucked as he fired, and the bullet caught the younger Wooley brother in the shoulder causing him to stagger backwards – but Wooley persisted in trying to draw his weapon and Sam fired a second time. This time the bullet hit the miner in the chest and knocked him backwards off his feet.

Too exposed where he stood, Sam dived for the cover of the open door of the lean-to, just as someone fired at him from inside the cabin. Whoever fired on Sam didn't intend making themselves a target, and no one showed at the cabin door so he could get a shot back at them.

'This is Sheriff Tom Mandall,' the local lawman shouted from his cover at the front of the cabin. 'You men inside come out with your hands in the air. We have the cabin surrounded, and there is no way out. You've got one minute to do as I bid or we'll burn the cabin down with you in it.'

This demand was met with silence, and Sam thought the two men inside the cabin were going to call the sheriff's bluff.

'You've got thirty seconds left,' the sheriff persisted. 'If you think I'm joking just stay where you are.'

'OK, we're coming out,' a voice announced from inside the cabin, but Sam couldn't see what was happening at the front because he was still watching the back door.

'Sam – there are two of them out here, and they are both unarmed,' the sheriff shouted. 'Can you see if the third one is out the back anywhere?'

Sam moved along to the back door and looked inside. He could see the two men through the open front door, and they were standing out in the open with their hands held high in the air. Moving back to where Glen Wooley lay in a crumpled heap near the lean-to, Sam checked him for signs of life – but there was none. He continued on around to the front of the cabin to find Tom standing in front of the two men covering them with his rifle.

'What happened around there?' he asked, as Sam joined them.

'I was just leaving the lean-to when Glen

Wooley got the jump on me. He had me cold, but he reholstered his sixgun and then drew against me. I was forced to shoot him. I just winged him, but he tried a second time – so I killed him.'

'You killed Glen!' Mike Wooley screamed, and lunged for Sam's throat with his arms extended.

Sam quickly sidestepped the outstretched arms, but Tom Mandall stopped the attack by clubbing the crazed miner across the back of his head with the barrel of his rifle.

Mike Wooley collapsed to the ground at Sam's feet and he sat there shaking his head dazedly. He put his hand to the back of his head and held the spot when the barrel of the rifle had come into contact with his skull.

'What the hell is this all about, Sheriff?' he groaned. 'Why did you bring this murdering scum down here to kill my brother?'

'We know you took those horses and the bodies from outside my office, Mike,' the sheriff replied. 'Sam came along as my deputy, and if your brother hadn't tried to draw on him he wouldn't be dead.'

'We never took any horses from outside your office,' the miner attested. 'The barman told you we were in the bar.'

'But you were seen talking to Martin Beller here, and he left the saloon soon after. That was around the time the horses and bodies disappeared, and your actions make it look very suspicious.'

'Since when is it a crime to talk to someone in a bar, Sheriff?' the miner asked in a hurt tone of voice. 'Martin invited me and Glen over to have a meal with him, and he left to come back here to get it ready.'

'You're a liar, Wooley,' Sam accused. 'If you are so innocent then what are those pack-horses doing in the lean-to?'

The miner raised his head, and the hatred he felt for Sam showed clearly in his eyes as he spat out his reply. 'Me and Glen found them standing by the side of the trail when we were riding over here. We intended to take them back into town and hand them over to the sheriff, but you came out here and killed my brother first.'

'He's lying through his teeth, Tom,' Sam protested.

'Was there any sign of the bodies in the lean-to with the horses?' the sheriff asked.

'No, but they would have got rid of them well before we arrived.'

'Then we've got no evidence against them,' the lawman informed him. 'And without evidence we can't make any charges stick.'

Sam bit back his frustration and realized that everything the old lawman had just said was true. Any charges brought against these men in a court of law would need to have some solid evidence to support them, or at least a witness to point the finger at them, but at present they had neither. He knew these men were guilty, but this time he had to give in to them.

'What do we do now?' he asked.

'We go back to town,' Tom Mandall replied. 'You go and get those pack-horses so we can take them with us.'

Sam did as he was bid and also retrieved his own mount from the bushes at the back of the cabin. Mike Wooley stood silently and watched him through narrowed eyes. He didn't have to speak to Sam to tell him what he was thinking, and the hatred that clearly showed in his eyes warned Sam that he would have to be watchful of the miner from now on.

EIGHT

Sheriff Tom Mandall climbed down from his horse and stood looking up at Sam, who had remained mounted. They were standing outside the front of the lawman's office, and they had yet to speak again about the shooting of Glen Wooley since leaving the miner's cabin some thirty-five minutes earlier.

'You are going to have to watch your back from now on,' the old lawman advised Sam. 'That Mike Wooley is pretty handy with a sixgun, and he'll be out shooting for you now that you've killed his brother.'

'I know that, Tom,' Sam replied pensively. 'But I had to kill his brother or he would have killed me.'

'We both know that, but it won't mean a thing to Mike Wooley. He's got a mean streak, and he's killed men for much less than what you did today.'

Sam shook his head defeatedly. 'I've really made a mess of this whole situation. Mike Hall sent me here to help his brother-in-law out of a spot of trouble, and so far all I've managed to do is make it a lot worse for both Harry and you, without helping either of you.'

'You're being too hard on yourself, Sam,' Tom Mandall assured him. 'You've done a lot more in one day to break this case apart than I've managed to do in six months.'

Before Sam could answer this, his attention was drawn to a wagon rattling along the street towards them carrying Igor Vlahov and Jim Carlton, headed straight for the law office.

'This will save me a trip out to the Golden Spirit Mine to see Vlahov,' the lawman announced cheerfully as he too spotted the wagon.

Igor Vlahov pulled the wagon to a halt outside the law office and passed the reins across to Jim Carlton. The foreman took them from his employer without speaking, but his eyes were locked on to Sam and they clearly showed the dislike he felt for the young Texas Ranger.

'I'm glad you decided to drop in, Igor,' Tom Mandall stated. 'I think we need to have a good long talk.'

'That sounds ominous, Tom,' Vlahov smiled amiably as he climbed down from the wagon.

'It won't be a social chat, Igor – it's much too serious for that,' the sheriff informed him. 'I think it would be best if you were to come inside before we start.'

The Russian nodded his head in acceptance and he then turned to face Jim Carlton. 'You go over to the general store and collect our supplies, Jim,' he instructed. 'I'll meet you over there as soon as I've finished here.'

The big man seemed less than impressed by this instruction from his employer. 'I'm staying right here,' he growled in return.

'No – you will do as I asked,' Igor Vlahov advised him coolly. 'I'll be over there in a few minutes to help you load up, so wait there for me.'

'Whatever you say, Mr Vlahov,' the mine foreman snarled sarcastically and viciously whipped the two horses that were pulling the wagon into action.

'He's a mean number, that one,' Tom Mandall opined as they watched the wagon move off along the street.

'Yes, I'm beginning to think you're right, Tom,' the mine owner conceded. 'Lately he's becoming more of a hindrance to me than a help.'

'You could always get rid of him,' Sam reasoned.

'I might just do that one day, but at the moment he has his uses,' he answered as he turned to look at Sam. Up until that moment he'd ignored the presence of the Texas Ranger sitting on the horse at the front of the law office, but now he focused his full attention on him. 'Maybe you'd like to take his place?'

'I'm not looking for a job,' Sam replied evenly. 'I'm here to help Harry Bird.'

A bemused grin lit Vlahov's face and his golden teeth sparkled in the sunlight. 'Harry Bird isn't the one who needs the help, son, it's us who need to be protected from that crazy old fool.'

'I agree he's not the easiest person in the world to get along with,' Sam reasoned. 'But he doesn't deserve to be shot at and harassed by your men.'

'Just hold on there a moment, youngster,' the mine owner demanded. 'You had better make sure of your facts before you go making accusations against me and my men, or you will answer to me.'

Before Sam could answer this threat Tom Mandall broke in on the exchange. 'Youngster, I think you should go and get yourself a cool drink, and leave Igor and me to talk over the events of today. Even better,

70

why don't you head back out to Harry's mine and then I'll ride out there to see you later on?'

Sam hated being brushed aside like this, but knew there was nothing to be gained by having a heated argument with Igor Vlahov out here in the middle of the street.

'I've got to go over and collect some supplies for Harry from the general store,' he advised the sheriff. 'Then I'll head on out to the mine.'

'You do that, son,' the sheriff encouraged, and watched as the young Texas Ranger started his mount off along the street towards the general store.

The front door of the store was wide open as Sam approached, and the mining company's wagon was standing unattended out the front. Sam pulled his mount to a halt outside the building and tied it off to the hitching rail and headed for the front door. He could hear a raised voice coming from inside the shop as he approached, and he entered the building cautiously. Inside he found Jim Canton and George Martin standing at the front of the counter, and Carlton had him held by the shirt-front as he spoke.

'What do you mean you didn't know he

was coming here, you little weasel?' the larger man growled. 'I told you what I'd do to you if you crossed me.'

Anger rose inside Sam when he saw the fear that showed on George Martin's face. 'It seems to me that you should learn to treat people with more respect,' he declared.

This challenge caused Carlton to release his grip and he turned to face Sam. 'And what the hell has it got to do with you?' he snarled.

'Seeing that I hate watching thugs like you push other people around, I suppose it's got a lot to do with me.'

'Maybe you think you're man enough to do something about it?' Carlton challenged as he moved towards Sam. ''Cause I'll rip you up into little pieces if I get my hands on you.'

Sam backed out the door into the street to give himself room to manoeuvre. Quickly he assessed his opponent and realized that he was taking on more than a handful with the giant mine foreman. Jim Carlton had bulging muscles in his upper arms and shoulders, and even with the excess weight he carried on his waistline, he would be no cream puff. The stance that Carlton offered as he fronted up to Sam showed that he was an experienced street-fighter, and that he would know how to look after himself in even the roughest of company.

He had got himself into a situation where he was going to be fighting for his life, so Sam forced himself to relax. When he had first joined the Texas Rangers some two years earlier, he had befriended a ranger who had once been a professional prize-fighter in England. This ranger had accidentally killed a nobleman in an exhibition fight in England, and he had been forced to flee his home country to escape hanging. In return for Sam having saved his life in a gun-battle, he had taught the youngster the art of prize-fighting – a skill that had come in handy more than once down in the badlands on the border between Texas and Mexico. Sam now knew that he was going to need all those skills if he hoped to defeat this giant man.

Sam struck the first blow after warily circling the foreman for several seconds. It was a good punch that landed high on Jim Carlton's cheek, and it brought a faint show of blood from the broken skin. Carlton brushed it aside as if it was a fly that had settled on him, and immediately countered with a right that sang past Sam's ear. Sam followed with a flurry of blows to his opponent's face, and although they brought more blood, they seemed as ineffectual as the first.

Carlton's fist exploded against the side of Sam's head and it felled him to the ground. He quickly followed up by landing several kicks to Sam's ribs, and the young ranger was forced to roll across the ground to get clear of his opponent so he could regain his feet.

The pain in Sam's ribs made him feel sick in the stomach, but he forced himself to ignore it as he moved in once again. Before he could land a punch, one of Carlton's glancing blows caught him on the side of his face, and blood began to flow from the cut it caused. Ducking low under the mine foreman's next punch, he brought his own fist up in a short, jarring blow that caught Carlton just below the right ear.

The man grunted in pain, but he merely shook off its effects, and then moved in on Sam once again. He drove home several good ones to Sam's head that caused the younger man to stagger under the onslaught. A smirk twisted Carlton's lips when he saw Sam's knees begin to buckle underneath him and almost go down.

A crowd had gathered around the two men

to watch the fight, and they shouted their encouragement to Sam as he attempted to shake the haziness from his battered mind. He continued to move backwards out of Carlton's reach to gain the precious seconds he needed to allow his mind to clear, but already Carlton was moving in for the kill. Sam turned his retreat into an attack, and surged forward to launch a flurry of punches that drove the foreman back on to his heels. A straight left from Sam caught the bigger man on the side of the jaw, and Carlton sagged at the knees. Sam then landed a hard right between his eyes, and the gathered crowd exclaimed aloud on hearing the crack of knuckle on bone – but Jim Carlton still refused to go down, and he backed away from Sam shaking his head weakly.

Sam was exhausted, and he had a ringing in his head that sounded like the pealing of church bells. He knew that he would have to finish this fight right now or suffer defeat. He forced himself to move in on the big man once again and landed several more punches to Carlton's face, and then sank his fist right up to his wrist into his midriff. This final blow had the effect of stopping the foreman in his tracks, and he stood with his arms hanging loosely at his sides sucking in gulps of air through his battered mouth. Sam looked at his opponent's bloodied face with pity, but this was short-lived as Carlton lowered his head and charged at Sam like an angry bull. This attack ended in disaster when Sam sidestepped him and brought his fist down hard behind Carlton's ear – and he crashed to the ground to lie still on his face.

Sam stood unsteadily, looking down at the unconscious man at his feet. The crowd that had gathered were cheering him wildly, but the ringing in his head blocked this out, and then everything went black as he collapsed unconscious to the ground.

NINE

Slowly, Sam drifted back into consciousness. He could feel the cooling touch of someone's hand on his forehead and he tried to open his eyes to see who it belonged to, but the effort caused pain to spear through his head and it made him groan loudly.

'You lie still and rest,' a soft voice advised him.

It was the voice of a young woman, and it sounded firm and husky. He tried to think who it belonged to, but his mind was too hazy to complete the thought. Once again he attempted to open his eyes, and this time he succeeded but all he could see was a distant glimmer of a light and dark shapes all around him. A sense of panic gripped him as he thought his eyesight had been damaged in the fight.

'I can't see,' he groaned aloud.

'The lamp's turned down,' the voice informed him, and the dark shapes took form when the girl reached across and turned the lamp up.

A sense of relief swept over Sam as he realized it was in fact after nightfall, and that he was lying in a bed, with an oil lamp lighting the room.

'I thought I was going blind,' he confessed to the girl seated on the bed beside him.

'You have a badly bruised face, and your eyes are swollen half-shut,' she revealed. 'You've also got concussion, and the doctor said you must rest up for a few days.'

Sam recognized the girl as Margaret Martin, whom he had met for the first time that morning on the road into Wilston. He tried to smile at her but his face hurt too much for him to continue the attempt.

Margaret laughed at this, and once again she placed her cooling hand on his battered face. 'You're lucky that you didn't lose some of those lovely teeth in that fight with Jim Carlton. When I first saw you I thought he had killed you.'

'The way my body feels at the moment he might've done me a favour by doing so,' Sam quipped.

'I'm glad he didn't,' the girl stated with a mischievous glint in her eyes. 'Then I wouldn't have you here in my bed, and at my mercy.'

Sam remembered the look she had given

him when they had first met that morning. She had managed to make him feel very uncomfortable with her forthright manner, and now he began to feel that way again.

'I'm sorry to put you out of your bed,' he apologized. 'If you could get someone to help me I'm sure I could make it across to the hotel.'

'There is no way you are getting out of this room now that I've got you trapped,' Margaret declared. 'I'm going to keep you here and nurse you until you are either fully recovered, or you die from the attention I give you.'

Sam didn't doubt for one moment that she meant what she had just said, and he had to admit that he found her very attractive. She was not backward in letting him know that she was interested in him, and he found her forthright manner pleasing. It was rare to meet a woman who was so straightforward in her approach, and she left little doubt about what she had planned for him. This thought caused Sam to flush with embarrassment, and the girl seemed to read his mind because she laughed loudly.

'It's all right,' she assured him. 'You'll be safe until you get over your injuries – then you can start worrying.'

'Have you heard anything from Harry Bird?' he asked, changing the subject quickly.

'The sheriff rode out to Harry's mine this afternoon to check on him, and to tell him about what happened to you. Tom said everything was quiet out there, and that Harry was his usual grumpy self. Tom also said to tell you that he will come and visit you as soon as you are well enough to have visitors.'

'What happened to Jim Carlton?'

'Igor Vlahov carted him out of town in the back of his wagon; he was still unconscious when they left.'

Sam couldn't think of any more questions to ask her, and he went quiet. He was beginning to feel tired, and his face muscles were hurting from all the talking.

Margaret Martin seemed to sense this and leaned forward to kiss him lightly on his bruised lips. 'You go to sleep now,' she instructed as she pulled the covers up to his chin. 'And I'll come and see you again in the morning.'

The girl then left the room and Sam drifted off into a deep sleep. He slept soundly throughout the night, and awoke the next day to find it was already mid-morning. Margaret

Martin was sitting on a chair beside the bed, and she smiled widely at seeing him awake.

'I thought you'd never wake up,' she declared.

Sam struggled to sit up in the bed, and although the pain in his ribs was still there it wasn't as bad as it had been the previous evening. Margaret moved across to help him sit up, and she then put several pillows behind his back and shoulders for support.

'Thank you,' he said through clenched teeth, and waited for the pain in his ribs to subside. 'You've been very kind to me and I really don't know how I'll ever be able to repay you.'

'Don't you worry about that,' the girl grinned impishly. 'I've already got a repayment plan in mind.'

Sam chuckled at this remark and the pain this caused to his battered face and body instantly made him regret this action. The bruising on his face had turned a deep purple in colour, and although he couldn't see it he could well imagine that he was no oil painting at the moment. 'I think I need to – er – wash – and soon,' he told the girl. 'If you could help me out of this bed I should be able to make it outside.'

'You will do no such thing,' she declared.

'Everything you need is over there in the corner.'

A large jug and dish stood on a dressing-table located in the corner of the room, with a chamberpot beside it. Sam knew he was in no position to argue with the girl, and gratefully accepted her assistance to climb out of the bed. He then noticed for the first time that he was dressed in a long nightshirt – and that he was completely naked underneath it.

'What happened to my clothes?' he asked through clenched teeth as he struggled to maintain his balance.

'I've washed them,' the girl informed him. 'I'll bring them up later when I've dried and ironed them.'

'You really didn't have to do that,' he assured her, and suddenly another thought occurred to him. 'Who undressed me and put me in the nightshirt?'

'I did,' she grinned. 'But you don't have to thank me – the pleasure was all mine.'

Sam flushed with embarrassment, and stood unsteadily beside the bed. He was finding the situation that he had put himself in by fighting Jim Carlton, very uncomfortable – and the fact that this girl had taken it upon herself to be his personal nurse was causing him a mixture of feelings that ranged from acute embarrassment to sexual desire.

Margaret left the room leaving Sam in private, and he was back in bed when she returned carrying a breakfast tray. She placed it on the bed beside him, and then reached across and tucked a napkin in the front of his nightgown.

'I can manage by myself,' Sam insisted, but the girl wasn't going to be stopped.

'You just sit there and relax,' she instructed. 'I've cooked you up some soft food so you won't go hurting your face by having to chew. All you have to do is open your mouth, and I'll spoon it in for you.'

Sam realized that he was in no condition to argue with her, and did as he was bid. She carefully spooned some soft boiled eggs into his mouth, and he found it wasn't too painful to chew and swallow. This process continued until the plate was completely emptied of its contents and she also helped him to drink a cup of sweet, lukewarm coffee.

Sitting back with satisfaction, the girl smiled as she eyed him. 'I haven't had that much fun in years – since I last played with my dolls.'

This comment did little to help Sam feel comfortable about his near-helpless state, and the expression on his face must have mirrored this thought.

'Don't worry, you're much more fun than my dolls ever were,' she assured him with a laugh. 'And I'd love to play dress-up with you sometime.'

Once again Sam felt flustered by the girl's forthright sexual manner, and to his relief there was a knock at the door to save him from her.

'Come in,' the girl ordered testily, annoyed at having her time with Sam interrupted.

An old man with shoulder-length grey hair entered the room, and he smiled on seeing the two young people sitting together on the bed. 'I'm sorry to disturb you two, but I'd like to have a look at this young man's injuries.'

'This is Doctor Myers, Sam,' Margaret announced as she stood up from the bed. 'He tended you yesterday while you were still unconscious. I'll leave you two together for ten minutes – no longer.'

The two men watched quietly as she collected up the breakfast tray and then left the room. 'She's a strong-willed young lady, that one,' the old doctor commented as he turned back to face Sam. 'You'll want to hope that she lets you out of here alive.'

'I'm planning on making a break for it as soon as I'm fit enough,' Sam assured him.

The old doctor moved across and placed his bag on the chair beside the bed before setting about examining Sam's bruised face. He clicked his tongue disapprovingly as he examined each of the dark purple areas on the younger man's face, and then probed his ribs until he finally stood back shaking his head sadly – thus causing Sam's eyes to widen with concern.

'Is there something wrong, Doc?' he asked anxiously.

'No – you'll mend OK,' the old doctor assured him. 'But you're a lucky young man. Your ribs aren't broken, but your body has taken a severe beating. I've been out to have a look at Jim Carlton this morning, and he's in much better condition than you – and you're supposed to have won the fight.'

Sam smiled with relief. 'There's an old saying that no one really wins a fight,' he contended. 'I guess this is a good example of the truth behind it.'

'You could be right, youngster,' the old doctor agreed as he turned to his bag. He pulled out a brown-coloured bottle and passed it across to Sam. 'Take some of that if the pain in your ribs becomes too unbearable – and you should be back on your feet again within a few days if you rest well.'

'What is this?' Sam asked as he turned the unlabelled bottle over in his hands.

'One of my patients makes it himself. I'm not sure what he puts in it, but it will either have a numbing effect on every part of your body when you drink it, or you should at least stop caring about the pain anyway.'

The old doctor then bid Sam good-day and left the room. It seemed to be only a matter of seconds before Margaret re-entered the room, and she moved across to sit down at the foot of Sam's bed.

'Doc told me that you will be OK, and that you haven't any broken ribs,' she informed him. 'So you should be up and about soon.'

Sam made a mental note to have a few words with Doctor Myers the next time he saw him. The examination of Sam's ribs by the old doctor had brought the pain on again, and he winced when he moved to make himself more comfortable in the bed.

'Are you all right?' the girl asked concernedly.

'Yes,' Sam replied slowly. 'I guess Doc's

poking around my ribs hasn't helped the bruising all that much.'

Margaret reached across and took the bottle that Sam still held in his hands. 'Doc told me that he left you some medicine for the pain – is this it?'

'Yes, but I'm not sure I should take any yet.'

'Nonsense,' the girl chided. 'Why put up with pain when you've got medicine that will stop it?'

She then moved across to the dressing-table and poured a couple of inches of the liquid into a glass. The liquid that ran from the bottle was a mild golden colour, and Sam wondered if the old doctor had been over-dramatizing its supposed effects.

Margaret passed the glass across to Sam, and he put it up to his lips and drank. He expected it to have a bite like moonshine whiskey, but instead it had a smooth sweet flavour. In fact, Sam quite liked it, and he handed the glass back for a refill. By the time he had downed the second glass, he could already feel a warm glow spreading through his body. His head began to feel fuzzy and he sat back to enjoy the sensation.

'Are you OK?' Margaret asked on seeing the lazy smile that played on his lips.

'I'm tired – I think I might take a sleep now,' he told the girl, and sat forward to allow her to remove the pillows from behind his back. He then slid down under the covers, and was sound asleep within seconds of his head hitting the pillow.

Margaret stood and looked down at his face as he slept. She sighed loudly as she reached out and pulled a strand of his long blond hair from his face. 'Why didn't I meet you years ago, Sam Brady?' she asked wistfully, before then turning and walking from the room.

When Sam awoke, it was dark outside and the room was once again lit by a lamp. He was alone in the room and he pushed himself up into a sitting position. The pain in his ribs had eased considerably, and he put this down to the deep sleep he'd experienced after drinking Doctor Myers' special medicine. He climbed from the bed and crossed the room to the washstand and was just returning to his bed when the door opened and Margaret Martin entered the room.

'You look much better after that sleep,' she informed him. 'Do you feel like eating?'

Sam was surprised to realize that he was ravenous, and he told the girl so. She responded by leaving the room, and returning some time later with a hot cooked meal. All the food was soft and easy to chew, and by the time he had finished he felt fully rejuvenated.

'I feel like getting up,' he stated, but a disapproving shake of the girl's head stifled this enthusiasm.

'You can get up tomorrow,' Margaret assured him. 'You might injure yourself if you get up too soon, so you will be better off taking your time.'

Sam realized that she was talking sense. Giving in to her wisdom, he settled back against his pillows. 'What time is it?' he asked.

'It's just after nine o'clock.'

'I guess it's too late to ask Tom Mandall to come over to have a talk?'

'I've told everyone that they should stay away from you until tomorrow. You need the rest, and it means that you are all mine until then.'

There was no sense in arguing with the girl, and Sam merely smiled in return. He tried to think of something to say to her but his mind was blank. Her green eyes glistened as she sat on the end of the bed watching his face, and this caused him to feel uncomfortable. As a means of hiding this discomfort, he reached for the bottle of painkilling medicine that was sitting on the table beside the bed.

A concerned look instantly registered on Margaret's face. 'Are you in pain again?' she asked.

'A little,' Sam lied, but he wanted anything but to have her sitting there waiting for him to make conversation.

Margaret took the bottle from his hands and poured some of the liquid into a glass. She then passed it across to him before picking up the tray from the end of the bed.

'You drink that while I take this tray back down to the kitchen,' she instructed.

Sam watched her leave the room before swallowing the contents of the glass in a single gulp. He then reached out and picked up the bottle and put it to his lips. He took a long swig and could feel the warmth of the alcohol as it spread through his body and began to numb his mind. He was giving in to its relaxing effects and snuggling down under the blankets when he heard Margaret re-enter the room.

'Are you OK?' she asked.

'Yes, I'm fine,' Sam mumbled. 'But I'm feeling a little sleepy so I might have a doze.'

Margaret reached out and pulled the

blankets up to his chin and kissed him gently on the lips, only this time the kiss was more prolonged. Her kiss became more urgent when she felt Sam starting to respond to her passion, and then she suddenly pulled away from him slightly breathless. She stood looking down at him for a moment, before reaching across and turning out the lamp.

Sam could hear the rustling of her clothing and then the covers of the bed were pulled back as she slid in beside him. She was completely naked, and willingly assisted in removing Sam's nightshirt. Sam told himself that this was madness, but it was too late to turn back. He reached for her and she came to him with a ferocity that was unlike anything he had ever experienced. His whole body became aware of her as she strained to him, and her hands at first kneaded his bruised body before her nails dug into his flesh. Her mouth moved fiercely against his, and suddenly her teeth sank into his lower lip and he tasted his own blood.

'Love me now, Sam. Love me now...'

Her voice was hoarse with desire, and moments later the battering his body had received during the previous day's fight was forgotten as he was swallowed up by the passion of the girl whose bed he shared.

TEN

George Martin entered the bedroom in the company of Tom Mandall. Both men stopped short on seeing Sam sitting up in the bed, and their expressions showed their surprise at what they saw.

'Hell – and you are supposed to have won the fight,' the sheriff commented drily. 'I'd hate to have seen you if you'd lost to Jim Carlton.'

'Is it really bad?' Sam asked anxiously.

The old lawman moved across to stand next to the bed and he leaned forward to closely examine Sam's face. 'I've seen worse,' he assured him. 'But then they'd been dead for two weeks.'

Sam smiled stiffly at this attempted humour from the lawman, but Margaret Martin didn't find it funny at all and she stood up from where she had been sitting at the foot of the bed and shook her head in disgust. 'You two can stay here with him for fifteen minutes and then I'll be back to throw you out,' she declared before walking from the room.

'She's got a temperamental disposition, that girl,' Tom Mandall attested. 'Does she take after your side of the family, George?'

'Hell, no,' he avowed. 'She's like her mother; Elizabeth's only related to me by marriage. Although I remember once when I was a kid when my mother...'

Sam relaxed back against his pillows and listened to the two older men talking. As their banter continued he let his mind drift back over the enjoyable night he'd spent with Margaret Martin. His body was still stiff and sore, but after spending the night with the girl he was amazed that he was still alive. Margaret was a demanding lover, and they had made love several times during the night. In the end he was too scared to move in case she woke up and decided that she wanted to make love again. When he finally awoke in the morning he found himself alone in the bed, and was surprised to find that he was disappointed she wasn't still there beside him. Margaret had returned to the room soon afterwards carrying his breakfast on a tray, and when he had asked for his clothes so he could get out of bed, she had refused to get them for him. Sam had remonstrated at this, so she had relented and promised to bring them to him at midday after he'd rested some more. Sam suspected she had an ulterior motive, but found he didn't mind if she did.

'You've got a contented smile on your face there, Sam,' Tom Mandall stated with a wicked glint in his eyes. 'Has Margaret done a good job nursing you?'

Sam flushed red; he didn't bother answering this jibe from the lawman, so George Martin added his own comments, 'She wouldn't let me or Elizabeth anywhere near this room after we carried you up here. Old Doc Myers was the only one who got in to see you, everyone else was banned.'

This conversation about Margaret Martin did nothing to help Sam feel any more comfortable about the fact that he was in the girl's bed, especially after what had happened between them during the night. 'Let's discuss something else,' he proposed self-consciously. 'How did your talk with Igor Vlahov go, Tom?'

The two old men grinned at the young man's obvious discomfort, but Tom Mandall saved him from further embarrassment by changing the subject. 'He denies knowing anything about the man you killed on the road into town and maintained that

Steve Wood was acting on his own when he shot at Harry. He also claimed that Mike and Glen came into town after completing their nightshift at the mine – and what they do in their own time has nothing to do with him.'

'Do you believe him?' Sam asked.

'I've got no evidence to the contrary,' the old sheriff replied, but on seeing the look of exasperation that this noncommittal reply brought to the younger man's face, he continued, 'Yes, I do believe him. I know Igor's a bit of a horsetrader, but I think he's honest enough.'

'Well I'll reserve my judgement,' Sam reflected. 'What do you think of Igor Vlahov, George?'

This question seemed to surprise George, who had been quietly listening to the two men. 'He's never done anything to me,' he admitted. 'He's always been pleasant enough, and the offer he made for my share of the mine was more than reasonable.'

Sam considered this reply realizing that he had a lot to learn about Igor Vlahov and his men. He had tried to keep an open mind about the Russian miner ever since he had first heard of him from Harry Bird, but so far the finger of blame seemed to point firmly in his direction.

'I'm getting out of this bed as soon as I get my clothes back,' he announced. 'And then I'm going to visit Igor Vlahov.'

'I wouldn't go doing that if I was you, youngster,' Tom Mandall warned. 'You've made yourself quite a few enemies out there, and you'll only be riding into trouble.'

Sam knew he was right. Since arriving at Harry Bird's mine some three days earlier, all he had managed to do was stir up the situation and lose the two bodies that were his only solid evidence. He had to admit to himself that there was little to be gained by riding out to the Golden Spirit Mine, and that it would be much more sensible for him to just back off and let things settle for a while.

'OK. I'll take your advice, Tom,' he finally relented. 'But I should go out to see how Harry is getting on.'

'That's a good idea, son,' the old lawman declared. 'And I think you'll find that everything will quieten down now, and that Harry will be able to get on with life in peace.'

'But that won't solve my problem though,' George Martin declared. 'I might ride out there with you Sam, and see if Harry has changed his mind about selling up.'

Sam readily agreed with this request, and the two men then set their departure for just after lunch. Further discussion was prevented when Margaret returned to the room and told the older men that it was time they left. It embarrassed Sam to see them hunted from the room like a couple of naughty children, but this embarrassment was soon forgotten when he heard the key being turned in the door lock, and saw the gleam that showed in her eyes when she turned to face him.

'I think it's time I had a close look at your bruising again,' she contended, as she moved across the room towards him, unbuttoning her blouse at the same time.

ELEVEN

Sam sat in the back of the wagon and waved to Margaret Martin as it moved off along the street. He was feeling a strange mixture of emotions as he watched her receding figure standing outside the front of the general store. He was relieved to be back on his feet and independent of her again, but he also felt a strong desire to be back in bed with her in his arms. Margaret had decided to stay behind to look after the store while her mother and uncle accompanied Sam out to Harry Bird's mine, but before he left she had made him promise that he would return to town that evening to spend the night with her once again.

Sam was still sore in the ribs, so he chose to ride in the back of the wagon being driven by Elizabeth Martin out to the mine, but he intended riding his horse back in to town. His saddle and gear were in the rear of the wagon beside him, and his horse was following along behind on a long lead. Elizabeth and George were sitting at the front of the wagon talking quietly as it rattled along the roadway, giving Sam the chance to survey the surrounding countryside in peace. The road followed the line of the Baron River towards the north, and every so often one of the cabins that had been built by the miners who had worked the river before the alluvial gold ran out, came into view. Some of these workings showed signs of recent digging, and several actually had men working on them. It was a hard life as a miner, and Sam didn't envy them one bit – but he had to concede that to work out in the open like these men did was much better than spending half your life under the ground like the Harry Birds and Igor Vlahovs of this world did.

The road swung away from the riverbank where it edged around a large outcrop of rocks and boulders that bordered the river, and this section of road was very rough. The wagon bounced along over the stones causing Sam to groan loudly from the pain that knifed through his ribs.

George Martin turned on his seat to check on the young Texas Ranger, and on seeing the pained look on his face he made a suggestion. 'Why don't you lie down flat on your back until we get through this rough section? It's only another couple of hundred yards or so before we get back on to the smooth dirt again.'

Sam did as he had suggested and there was an instant easing of the pain in his ribs, as he lay back and waited for the lurching and rattling of the wagon to subside. Suddenly, he heard a cracking sound over the noise of the wagon, and also heard a cry of pain from George Martin. He looked up just in time to see the old man slump over the side of the wagon and disappear from view – and then Elizabeth Martin was also hit. She fell backwards into the wagon on top of Sam, and he was forced to push her aside before he could check her condition. She had been hit in the right side of the head with a rifle bullet, and was dead.

Pulling his rifle from its saddle boot where it lay in the back of the wagon with the rest of his equipment, Sam quickly ran the situation through his mind. Both George and Elizabeth had been hit by bullets fired off to their right, so this meant the ambusher was hiding in cover on that side of the road. The wagon was still moving along at an easy pace, and Sam hoped that it would soon be clear of the danger offered by the bushwhacker, but this hope was dashed when he heard more rifle-fire and the wagon suddenly came to a lurching halt. The horses pulling the wagon had been shot, and he also realized from the sound of the rifle-fire that there was more than one gun. It was clear to him now that they knew he was in the back of the wagon, and that they were intent on killing him as well.

Looking around for a means of escape, Sam weighed up his options. The wagon had wooden sides of around twenty-four inches high that offered him good cover – but there was no tail-board, so he was vulnerable to rifle-fire if someone decided to move around behind him. He also realized that it would be suicide to show himself above the side of the wagon in an attempt to return fire, so this left him with little choice but to try to get out of the wagon and to make for the cover of the surrounding scrub. He examined the inside of the wagon in search of anything that might assist him to escape without exposing himself and something caught his eye. The wagon was an old freight wagon, and it had side-panels that were hinged so they could be lowered to allow the easy side-loading of goods – and these hinged panels could be released from inside the wagon. Sam reached out and grasped the head of the drop-bolt that fastened the side-panel to the head-board, but it was rusted into place. Using the butt of his rifle he hammered at the drop-bolt until it finally slid out of its fixing points, and he then pushed the side-panel outwards and let it swing down against the side of the wagon with a crash.

Even before the panel had come to rest, Sam had swung himself over the side of the wagon and was moving forward to take cover behind the front wheel. He took a quick look back over his shoulder and saw the body of George Martin lying in an untidy heap further back down the road. He had no doubt that the old miner was dead – but he pushed this from his mind as he forced himself to concentrate on the bush-whackers waiting across the track. They were positioned in amongst the smaller boulders near the edge of the rocky outcrop, and it would be suicidal for him to attempt to return their fire from his position behind the wagon.

Several bullets thudded into the side of the wagon as if to reinforce this thought, and Sam listened to the rifle-fire with interest. It confirmed his belief that there were only two rifles firing on him, and with this in mind he began to formulate a plan. He turned his attention to the horses at the front of the wagon, and noted that the right horse was down in its harness and was dead, but the left horse was still standing unharmed. It was moving around nervously in its harness, but was held in check by the dead weight of its companion.

Sam's plan was to use the surviving horse to shield his run for the cover of a group of boulders located on the opposite side of the track in an attempt to prevent George and Elizabeth's killers from escaping. He moved forward and released the horse from the harnessing pole, and instantly it started forward. With rifle in hand, Sam ran beside the horse as it angled across the roadway, and this move caught the ambushers off-guard. He managed to make it most of the way across before they finally reacted and opened up with a withering burst of rifle-fire. The horse whinnied in pain as bullets thudded into its body, and it then stumbled and fell lifeless to the ground.

Sam had to make a run for it across the remaining distance while fully exposed to the ambushers' fire. Bullets buzzed past his body, and several more sang past his head as he sprinted for cover, but he made it to safety and dived behind the boulders where he lay breathing heavily.

The rifle-fire instantly ceased, and Sam drew his feet up under him and crawled forward through the rocks until he was sure he was fully screened from their view. He estimated their hiding position was about 140 feet from his position, and it was all open ground between them. The bush-whackers had the upper hand because they knew exactly where he was hiding, but for Sam to attempt to take a look in the hope of locating their position would mean that he would stand a good chance of being shot – so he decided instead to find a way to draw their fire away from his position long enough to locate them.

Placing his hat on the end of a stick, Sam raised it above the edge of the rock that he was hiding behind, and no sooner had it cleared the edge than they opened fire again. Instantly the hat was hit, and it flew off the end of the stick to land on the ground some feet away from him.

'They really know how to use those rifles,' Sam muttered to himself as he retrieved his hat and placed it on the end of the stick again. He then repeated the action of raising it over the edge of the rock, and once again the riflemen opened up and the hat went flying.

'That's stirred them up enough for now,' he chuckled as he retrieved his hat again. He settled back against the rock and then set about unwinding a strip of leather from around the band of his hat. When the strip was completely unwound it measured over a yard in length, and Sam cut it into two pieces with a small folding knife that he pulled from his pocket. He put the shorter of the two pieces aside before reaching out and taking hold of a bush that grew in behind the rock. He tied the longer piece of leather to the stem of the bush about three quarters of the way up from the bottom, and then drove his knife into the ground and bent the bush over towards it. After quickly tying the other end of the leather-strip to the handle of the knife, he released the bush and checked that it was holding securely. The young man then retrieved the shorter piece and used it to tie a long stick to the stem of the bush. This stick protruded out past the top of the bush, and Sam set its length so it would be higher than the edge of the boulder when it was completely upright. He then checked that the whole setup was secure before placing his hat on the end of the stick.

'I hope this works,' he declared as he piled up some dry twigs under the leather near where it was tied to the handle of the knife, and he then fished a match out of his pocket. He picked his rifle up in his left hand, and lit the match with his other hand before putting it to the pile of twigs. The twigs began to burn fiercely, but the flame was several inches short of reaching the leather strip but the heat was rising directly up to it and it began to smoulder.

Satisfied, Sam crawled off through the boulders and took up position some twenty feet from where he was first hiding. He knew that he would only have one chance to make his plan work, and it would require quick reflexes and good shooting if he was going to pull it off.

From where he was positioned, Sam could see the leather slowly smouldering away under the heat from the small fire. He pulled his legs up under him and held his rifle ready in his hands as he watched the strip, and waited for it to break. It seemed like an eternity before it finally broke, and the bush whipped back up into its upright position and flicked the hat in the air. Sam was already coming to his feet as the hat rose into the air, and he managed to brace his rifle across the top of the rock just as the ambushers fired at his diversion. He could see the riflemen positioned amongst the boulders at the edge of the rocky outcrop, and they both had their heads and shoulders exposed as they fired at the hat.

Sam quickly took aim on the nearest man with his rifle and squeezed the trigger. The gunman fell from his view and Sam was already moving his aim to the second gunman. This man was moving his aim on to Sam at that same moment, and both men fired simultaneously. The bullet from the gunman's rifle hit the rock inches from Sam's face and showered him with sparks and splinters of stone as the bullet ricocheted away past him. The young Texas Ranger ducked his head instinctively, and by the time he refocused on the gunman's position he could no longer see him.

Sam wasn't sure if his bullet had found its mark on the second gunman, and this made him feel uneasy. The gunman could be over there playing possum, and Sam wasn't keen on having to find out. He was positive that he'd hit the first gunman, but it was going to be risky for him to find out if he'd hit the second, whom he had recognized as being

Mike Wooley, the man whose brother he had killed only two days before.

The sound of a horse being ridden away at speed from the direction of the river caused Sam to break cover and run out into the roadway. He put his rifle to his shoulder as Wooley broke from the cover of the trees on the riverbank, and headed off along the road at a full gallop. Sam fired at him, and levered a fresh shell in the rifle before firing a second time. He knew that both shots had been wide of their target, and he swore savagely at himself for having missed.

Moving back along the roadway, Sam made his way over to the outcrop of rocks where the gunmen had been hiding. He moved in amongst the rocks and boulders, and soon found what he was seeking. The body of Martin Beller lay on the ground behind a large rock. The miner had been hit in the head with the bullet from Sam's rifle, and he was dead. He lay with his eyes wide open, and was staring up at the sky, but the red dot of a third eye that showed in the middle of his forehead revealed that he saw nothing.

Sam quickly checked the area to make sure that there was no one else hiding in amongst the rocks, but all he found was

Martin Beller's horse. Mike Wooley had made a clean break for it, and this angered Sam. 'I think me and Mike Wooley have a lot of unfinished business to sort out,' he asserted as he made his way back towards the wagon.

TWELVE

Sam guided his horse over to the side of the roadway and sat watching the distant mine workings. He had followed Mike Wooley's trail all the way from the ambush site to the Golden Spirit Mine. Wooley's trail had been easy to follow because his horse's hooves had cut imprints into the surface where it had been galloped at full speed all the way to the mine workings. It had taken Sam some time to load the bodies of Martin Beller and George Martin into the wagon beside that of Elizabeth Martin, but he had completed this task before heading out after Mike Wooley. He had considered riding back into town to enlist the help of Sheriff Tom Mandall in the hunt for Wooley, but had rejected this idea when he realized that it would give the miner too much of a head start in making good his escape.

It was still mid-afternoon, and Sam could see several men working at the entrance to the mine shaft. The single figure of a man could be seen standing at the front of the buildings located on a rise behind the stamp mill, and Sam recognized Igor Vlahov. The mine owner was standing watching Sam, and he made no effort to move when the young Texas Ranger started his horse forward again. Sam followed the roadway past the silent stamp mill, and then steered his mount up towards the mine buildings.

'What can I do for you, young man?' Vlahov asked warily, as Sam pulled his horse to a halt in front of him.

'I'm looking for Mike Wooley,' he replied bluntly.

'He's not here,' the mine owner advised him.

Sam ran his gaze around the mine workings in the hope of seeing Wooley's horse, but when he failed to spot it he turned back to face the mine owner. 'I know that Wooley came this way about fifteen minutes ago,' he stated coolly. 'So he must be around here somewhere, and if you're not going to tell me where he is I'll search this place until I find him.'

Vlahov's normally smiling face was now devoid of humour as he answered, 'You'd better have a damn good reason for coming here and trying to throw your weight around, young man,' he warned. 'Because if you don't, I'll have my men throw you off this site with more than just a few bruises to remember me by.'

This threat incensed Sam and he was tempted to call the mine owner's bluff, but he decided instead to see how he would react to the news of George Martin's death. 'I'm looking for Wooley because he just shot and killed George Martin, and his sister-in-law, Elizabeth. I saw Wooley riding away from the ambush towards this mine, and I don't intend leaving here until I get him.'

The look that registered on the mine owner's face was one of disbelief. His mouth dropped open, and he shook his head slowly from side to side. 'Why the hell would Mike want to kill George and Elizabeth?' he asked.

'I thought you might be able to tell me that,' Sam replied evenly. 'Now, where is Wooley?'

This pointed remark caused anger to once again register on the mine owner's face, but he managed to control his temper as he replied, 'I have no idea why Wooley would want to kill George and Elizabeth – and as to where he is I really can't tell you. He rode in here some time back and packed his gear before heading out again. When I asked him what he was doing, he told me to mind my own business – and that's exactly what I did.'

'Which direction did he go?' Sam probed.

'He crossed to the other side of the river and headed towards town – so I naturally assumed he was going in to Wilston.'

Sam wasn't sure whether to trust the mine owner or not. He couldn't help but like his open friendly manner, but he had met men before today who were quite capable of giving you a friendly smile while at the same time sliding a knife between your ribs.

'I know you don't trust me,' the mine owner remarked, as if reading the younger man's thoughts, 'all I can do is assure you that I didn't have anything to do with the deaths of George and Elizabeth, and that I'll do anything I can to help you bring Mike Wooley to justice if he is responsible.'

'Did anyone talk to Wooley while he was here at the camp?' Sam asked, deliberately ignoring Vlahov's assurances.

He hesitated a moment before answering. 'Jim Carlton went over to see him – but I don't think anyone else spoke to him.'

Sam considered this news, but decided there was nothing to be achieved by confronting Carlton at this time. He knew the situation between himself and the mine foreman was very explosive at the present time, so he chose to keep clear of him until he had some firm evidence.

'Jim Carlton is over in the bunk-house right now,' Igor Vlahov announced as if reading his mind once again. 'He's still badly bruised from that beating you gave him – and he hates you intensely.'

'I don't particularly like him either,' Sam assured the mine owner. 'And I'll see him when the time is right.'

'Can I come with you to help hunt down Wooley?' Vlahov asked abruptly.

'I'm not going after him right now,' the young ranger replied. 'I've got to take George and Elizabeth's bodies into town first, and then I'll get out after him.'

'Then I'll come and help you with that,' Vlahov insisted, and then turned and disappeared into the cabin before Sam could respond. It was only a matter of seconds before he reappeared fastening his gunbelt around his waist.

'We're going to need a couple of horses that can pull the wagon,' Sam informed him. The mine owner responded by walking off around the side of the building, and Sam could hear him shouting orders to his men.

Igor Vlahov soon returned riding his

horse, and leading two heavily built horses on a long lead. Sam nodded his head in approval before turning his mount and starting towards the south. Vlahov drew in beside him, and they had barely covered a hundred yards before he spoke out. 'I know that you still think I'm behind what Mike Wooley did to George and Elizabeth,' he announced openly. 'All I can do is maintain my innocence, and level with you about why I was after Harry and George's mine. You see, my mine produces a good yield of gold, but I know that the majority of the gold found in the river to the south of here didn't come from this side of the hill. There's no doubt that some of it came from the exposed ore that we found in this valley, but I'm now positive that the motherlode is located in Harry Bird's canyon. I did offer both Harry and George an equal partnership if they would consider combining our operations – but Harry rejected that offer along with my offer to buy them both out.'

Realizing that Igor was intent on assuring him of his innocence, Sam refused to allow his judgement to be influenced by the personable mine owner. The stench of culpability hung around the Russian, and until he could prove his innocence Sam intended keeping him at arm's length. 'I'm keeping an open mind until we can get the truth from Mike Wooley,' he informed him. 'And until then you are wasting your time trying to convince me of anything else.'

The Russian shrugged his shoulders before replying, 'At least you don't beat around the bush,' then rode on in silence.

The two men rounded the bend in the road and found the wagon still where Sam had left it. They also saw a mule standing beside the wagon, and the figure of a man watching them with a shot-gun in his hands. Both men pulled their mounts to a halt, but Sam recognized Harry Bird so he started his horse forward once again.

'Hold it right there, youngster – or I'll blow you into little pieces,' the old miner growled, causing the young ranger to stop his horse, and frown at this threat.

'What the hell are you on about, Harry?' he asked.

'It's pretty obvious to me that you've thrown in with that murdering Russian and his men, and you've gone and killed my partner.'

Sam shook his head in disbelief. 'You're making a big mistake, Harry,' Sam warned. 'I didn't kill George and Elizabeth, but I did kill that man lying in the back of the wagon with them. He was one of the men who ambushed them, and I killed him before riding out after the one who escaped.'

Doubt registered on Harry's face, and he glanced at the bodies lying in the back of the wagon. 'Are you telling me that Vlahov was the one who got away?'

'No, Harry. Igor says he had nothing to do with George and Elizabeth's murder. But I do know that Mike Wooley was the second gunman, and that he has gone back into Wilston. Igor came out here to help me get the wagon and bodies back into town.'

Sam watched while the old miner lowered his shot-gun, and then turned in the saddle and signalled Igor to ride forward with the other two horses.

Harry Bird seemed to suddenly lose his strength, and he slumped back against the wagon shaking his head dejectedly as he looked down at the body of his old partner.

'Are you OK?' Sam asked, as he dismounted. He received a sad nod of the head in reply and found himself feeling sorry for him. He had been forced to bury his own partner, Tate Sharp, not two years before, when he had been killed by a gang of outlaws they had been trailing. Sam and Tate had been partners in the deadly trade of bounty-hunting, and over the four years they had spent together they had developed a friendship that was unshakeable. Sam had buried his old partner by the trail-side before then setting out to bring the killers to justice and, by the time he had finished his task, several of them had chosen to die under his guns rather than face the hangman's noose.

With Igor Vlahov's help, Sam used the horses to drag the dead ones clear of the roadway, before then harnessing them to the drawbar of the wagon. Harry sat on the ground beside the wagon not offering to help, then finally spoke out when Sam stopped next to him.

'I killed George,' he confessed. 'I killed him as surely as if I pulled the trigger myself.'

'That's a crazy thing to say, Harry,' Sam remonstrated. 'You didn't know those men were going to kill him.'

'He wanted to sell the mine, and I wouldn't let him,' he explained. 'If I'd sold out when he wanted to none of this would've happened.'

'It's too late for recriminations, Harry,' Sam stated. 'You would be better served putting your energies into helping me get this wagon back into town, and then I can get out after Mike Wooley.'

This statement took several seconds to penetrate the old man's misery before he turned to face Sam with renewed energy. 'You're absolutely right, youngster,' he conceded. 'I'll go into town with you, and then we can get out after Wooley together.'

This wasn't exactly what Sam had meant but, as it had achieved the desired effect, he didn't bother saying anything to the old man. 'How about you heading for town with the wagon, and after I find this dead man's horse I'll catch up with you.'

'OK,' Harry agreed. 'But I'm warning you to keep that murdering Russian away from me, or I'll be tempted to do to him what he did to George.'

Sam knew that he would be wasting his breath by trying to talk sense to the old miner, so instead he agreed to do as Harry demanded. 'Igor will be riding into town with me, so just calm down.'

Harry Bird muttered something under his breath that Sam couldn't quite make out, before moving around to the rear of the wagon to tie off his mule. Then he climbed up on to the driver's seat, and masterfully wheeled the wagon around and started it off along the road towards town.

Sam stood beside Igor and watched the

wagon's trailing dust for a moment before speaking. 'We'd better see if we can find that horse, and then we'll have to hightail it if we hope to catch Harry before he reaches town.'

THIRTEEN

Sam and Igor caught up with Harry just as he was entering the outskirts of Wilston, and they fell in behind the wagon. The sight of the returning wagon and its accompanying riders drew furtive glances from the locals but no one attempted to speak to them as they made their way towards the centre of town.

An uneasy feeling settled over Sam as he considered this reaction. He would have expected some of them to at least show an interest in the sight of the Martins' wagon returning to town in company of the two miners who were supposedly sworn enemies, but so far their reaction had been guarded. Sam could understand that they might not want to get involved but he also knew that human nature usually drives people to show a lot more interest than this – and he began to suspect that there was more behind it than just plain disinterest.

Harry Bird stopped the wagon in front of the sheriff's office, and Sam pulled his horse to a halt behind it and dismounted. He stood looking around, and noticed the distinct lack of people moving around near the centre of town. A shiver ran up Sam's spine when he thought he saw something move in amongst the shadows of an alleyway further up the street, and he guessed that there might be someone hiding in there watching them. The uneasiness that the young Texas Ranger was feeling also seemed to be affecting Igor Vlahov where he was waiting on his horse at the rear of the wagon, and he raised a quizzical eyebrow at Sam when their eyes met.

Sam merely shrugged his shoulders in reply, before tying his horse's reins to the hitching rail and walking across to the office door. He knocked loudly and then waited, but there was no answer from the old lawman.

'He's probably gone fishing,' Harry Bird growled from the driver's seat of the wagon.

Sam ignored this sarcastic remark, and knocked on the door once again. This time he heard a muffled voice call out for him to enter, so he reached for the battered brass doorhandle.

'Are you there, Tom?' he enquired as he eased the door open and peered into the gloomy darkness of the office.

'He's here all right, Brady – but he's going to be dead if you try anything fancy,' a voice warned and, as Sam's eyes adjusted to the gloomy interior of the office, he saw Mike Wooley standing beside a battered and bruised Tom Mandall, a sixgun pressed against the sheriffs temple.

'Let the sheriff go, Wooley,' Sam demanded. The sheriff's arms were tied at the wrists with rope and there was a gag tied across his mouth. 'You're only going to make things a lot worse for yourself if you go hurting a lawman.'

'I'm going to more than just hurt you, Brady,' Wooley snarled. 'I'm going to shoot you down like a dog for killing my brother.'

'I told you that I killed your brother in a fair fight,' Sam protested. 'He drew on me first, and I was forced to kill him.'

'My brother was skilled with a gun, and you expect me to believe that you beat him in a fair fight,' the outlaw scoffed. 'You killed him, Brady, and now you're going to die for it. My brother was quick but I'm even quicker – and I'm going to give you the chance to draw against me. Now, back out and tell your friends to leave their weapons in a heap outside the door – and then you

125

wait for me in the middle of the street.'

Standing his ground, Sam made no effort to do as Wooley had instructed. 'Your brother was a fool who died for no reason,' he stated. 'If he hadn't forced me to draw on him he would still be alive. So don't you go making the same mistake – it's not worth it.'

Sam waited for a reaction from the outlaw, and his heart sank when he heard the hammer being cocked on the gun that was being held to Tom Mandall's temple. Realizing that he might have pushed the man too far, he quickly spoke out. 'OK, Wooley. I'll do as you say,' he yielded, and was relieved when he saw the man ease the hammer closed. There was nothing to be gained by trying to talk Mike Wooley out of his planned action, and Sam conceded that a gunfight would at least give both himself and Tom Mandall a chance to survive.

'Go outside and do as I said,' the outlaw directed once again. 'And if there's any hint of a trick I'll shoot the sheriff.'

Sam turned and walked back out into the street to find Igor Vlahov had already dismounted and was now standing at the back of the wagon with his gun in his hand – but Harry Bird was sitting on the driver's seat of the wagon with his shot-gun levelled on the Russian.

'I've got this one covered, youngster,' the old miner growled. 'And if he makes one wrong move I'll blow him to pieces.'

'This is my fight with Mike Wooley, Harry,' Sam informed him irritably. 'Igor's got nothing to do with it, and neither have you – so give me that damn shot-gun before you end up shooting yourself with it.'

The old miner lowered his weapon and passed it across but the look that registered on his face showed that he was far from pleased with the dressing-down that he had just received.

Igor Vlahov also handed over his weapon. 'I guess I should thank you for believing that I've got nothing to do with this,' he declared.

'I only said you've got nothing to do with my fight with Mike Wooley,' Sam corrected, and saw the smile slide from the mine owner's face. 'I still haven't made my mind up about the rest – but for now you and Harry can move across to the other side of the street and make sure you stay out of this fight.'

Sam waited until the two older men had done as he had bid, then pushed them from his mind as he laid their weapons outside the sheriff's door. Moving out into the street he took up position as he had been instructed. While he waited for Wooley to make an appearance, he dropped his hand to his sixgun and eased it in its holster. The feel of the weapon in his hand had a calming effect on him as it slid in and out of the well-oiled holster, and Sam began to feel relaxed and confident.

Movement at the door of the office caught Sam's eye, and he saw Tom Mandall stumble out through the doorway into the street. Mike Wooley was directly behind him with his sixgun held against the back of the lawman's head, and the outlaw pulled him up short by tugging on the back of the lawman's shirt.

Mike Wooley stood for a moment looking up and down the street to check that everything was to his liking, before turning his attention back to Sam. 'Move on up the street,' he instructed the younger man, and indicated the direction off to his left.

This positioned Sam with his back to the mouth of the alleyway where he had earlier seen movement in amongst the shadows, and he now knew that there was someone hiding in the alleyway who would be helping Wooley in the gunfight. This thought caused a shiver to once again run up Sam's spine, as he realized that he'd not only have to beat Wooley to the draw, but also have to try to cover the person in the alleyway before they could get a shot at him.

Mike Wooley waved his arm, and a man carrying a rifle walked out of the saloon. This man stopped at the side of the street and aimed his rifle at Igor Vlahov and Harry Bird. Seemingly satisfied with these arrangements, Wooley pushed Tom Mandall to the ground before walking out into the street and facing up to Sam. A knowing smile played on the outlaw's lips, smug in the knowledge that his opponent had little hope of surviving the gunfight – whatever his speed.

Sam pushed this thought from his mind as he forced himself to concentrate on the situation before him. He knew that he had little hope of taking out both Wooley and the gunman in the alleyway behind him – so he resigned himself to focusing his efforts on beating Wooley and then trying to take on the second gunman standing at the front of the saloon. This would all but guarantee his own death, but it would at least give Igor and Harry a chance to survive.

Wooley seemed relaxed and confident as

he stood watching Sam. He seemed to be in no hurry to push the fight to a climax, and a smile played on his lips as he casually eyed the young Texas Ranger. His hand was tensed into a claw where it hovered close by the butt of his sixgun, but Sam concentrated on the outlaw's face.

When the move came it was explosive, and Mike Wooley's grin turned into a grimace as his hand plucked his sixgun from its holster. His draw was a blur of movement, and there was a boom as he fired his weapon – but his was the second sixgun to fire. It was all over in a split second, and Mike Wooley was already crumpling to the ground when another shot crashed out.

No sooner had Sam fired his first shot that had hit Mike Wooley squarely in the chest, than he moved his aim to the gunman standing at the front of the saloon. He fired a second time, and the bullet hit the gunman in the side of the head. Sam expected any moment now to feel the impact of a bullet in his back fired by the gunman in the alleyway, but to his surprise he heard a rifle-shot but felt no impact. He spun around and threw himself to the ground believing the rifleman had missed him with his first shot, and that he now had a slim chance of taking him out before he could fire again – but to his surprise he saw that the rifleman had slumped to the ground at the mouth of the alleyway, and wasn't moving.

The adrenalin that pumped through Sam's veins made him shake involuntarily as he climbed back to his feet, and he stood looking at the gunman lying at the alley-mouth with disbelief written on his face. He then looked around for the source of the rifle-shot that had saved his life, but he could see nothing.

'Are you all right, youngster?' Harry Bird asked as he hurried across towards Sam.

'Yes, I'm OK, Harry,' Sam assured him as he looked around at the bodies lying in the street, and then thanked the Lord that he wasn't one of them.

Igor Vlahov seemed far less concerned about the young Texas Ranger's condition than Harry Bird was. He headed directly across the street to where Tom Mandall was lying on the ground, and was now busily untying him.

'Did you happen to see where that shot come from that hit the gunman in the alley-way?' Sam asked Harry Bird.

'Hell no,' the old miner replied. 'I didn't even see who shot Wooley. You were dead meat until someone shot him for you.'

Sam looked at the old miner incredulously. He thought for a moment that he was joking, but the look on Harry's face told Sam that he was serious.

'I shot Wooley!' Sam stated irritably. 'I also shot that gunman standing at the front of the saloon covering you and Igor with a rifle.'

A confused frown knitted Harry's brow, but his reply was quick. 'I knew that – I'm not stupid you know. I was just kidding. Now, hadn't we better check these *hombres* and make sure none of them are still kicking?'

'OK, Harry. You go check that body over in the alley-mouth, and I'll check the other two,' Sam directed before making his way over to Mike Wooley's body. He checked him for signs of life, but found none, and then moved across to the body of the gunman at the front of the saloon and found the same result.

'I thought he had you, Sam,' Tom Mandall admitted as he and Igor joined him at the front of the saloon. 'Hell, Mike was quick on the draw – but you were faster.'

'It was a close thing, and if it hadn't been for the person who shot that gunman in the alley-mouth I'd be dead right now,' Sam assured him. 'Did either of you two see who shot him?'

Both men shook their heads in reply. Further discussion was forestalled when Tom Mandall noticed the local town residents were starting to make their way out into the street to view the results of the gunfight.

'Let's get these bodies on to the wagon, and then over to Doc Myers' surgery before the whole population of the town turns out to have a look at them,' the sheriff suggested, and his companions nodded their agreement.

It was nearly an hour later before Sam finally left the other three men at the sheriff's office, and made his way towards the store. He had assisted the sheriff to move the bodies over to the doctor's surgery, and then sat down to relate the details of the murder of George and Elizabeth to the town sheriff. Sam was now on his way to tell Margaret Martin about her mother's death, a task that he was not looking forward to. On entering the store he saw the girl sitting on a stool behind the counter eating a stick of liquorice, and when she looked up she beamed a smile at him.

'You've caught me out with my only vice,' she grinned, and Sam's heart sank as he realized that he must destroy her happy mood.

'I need to talk to you in private, Margaret,' he stated, and turned around to close and lock the door behind him before then moving over to where she was waiting at the counter.

A bemused smile played on the girl's lips as she misread Sam's motive. 'All right, I do have one more vice – but you will have to wait until Mother returns to look after the shop before we can do anything about it.'

Sam felt embarrassed by this forthright remark from the girl, and was momentarily at a loss for words. 'Your mother and uncle won't be coming back here,' he informed her hesitantly.

'What is that supposed to mean, Sam?' she asked. 'Of course they will be coming back.'

Sam took a deep breath to steady his nerves. His eyes were locked on to the girl's face, and he could already see the panic starting to show in her eyes. 'Your mother is dead, Margaret. Both she and George were shot dead when we drove right into the middle of an ambush on the way to Harry's mine.'

Tears welled up in the girl's eyes, and she forlornly searched Sam's face for some sign that might indicate that he was joking – but she found none.

Sam quickly moved around the shop counter and took her into his arms as she broke down in tears. He felt powerless to help her in her grief, and even the words he muttered to her seemed shallow. 'I'm sorry, Margaret,' he proffered. 'I really am sorry.'

The two young people stood there for some time in each other's arms before the girl's sobs finally began to ease. Sam took this as a sign that she was recovering and eased her back in his arms so he could look at her face. 'I've locked the door, so let's go upstairs and you can have a lie-down,' he suggested.

The girl nodded her head without meeting his gaze, and she allowed him to lead her away from the counter. He took her upstairs to her bedroom and helped her lie down on the bed. He then sat down beside her and leaned across to kiss her on the cheek, but as he went to pull away she quickly reached out and wrapped her arms around his neck to stop him.

'Don't leave me, Sam,' she begged in a broken voice. 'I need you with me.'

Sam eased back down on to the bed beside her. 'I'll stay here as long as you need me,' he assured her – but her response to this was totally unexpected.

'Make love to me, Sam,' she implored. 'I need to be held and loved right at this moment – and I want you to do it for me.'

This plea left Sam speechless. He hadn't expected such a request at a time like this, but this girl wasn't any normal girl. She was a strong-willed person who showed that she had a mind of her own, and if she needed him to help her through the trauma of her mother's death, then he couldn't deny her. He reached out and took her in his arms, their lips crushing together in a long kiss. They then went on to make love – not the hungry and wild love they had experienced the previous night, but a more gentle and caring love that left them both spent and exhausted.

FOURTEEN

Sam rolled over in the bed and opened his eyes, then sat up and stretched luxuriously. The sun was already streaming in through the bedroom window, and there were birds chirping happily in the trees outside. It was now two days since the deaths of George and Elizabeth Martin, and Margaret seemed to have her grief well under control. After the first night when she had clung to Sam throughout the dark hours, she had then settled down and was now able to speak about her mother's and uncle's deaths without breaking down and crying. She had asked Sam to tell her the full details of the ambush, and after he explained just how close he had come to dying and that his bruised ribs had actually saved his life, she had hugged him to her chest and thanked God that he had been spared.

The funeral of George and Elizabeth had taken place the previous day in the town cemetery. Over thirty people had attended, and even Igor Vlahov had made an appearance, but had wisely stayed well back from the main group of mourners – and he had left straight after the service without speaking to anyone.

As there was no church or minister in the town, the president of the Local Business Association, James Morgan, had read the sermon over the open graves.

Harry Bird had stood quietly throughout the service, and had declined a request to say a few words over George Martin's grave. The death of his friend and partner seemed to have visibly shaken the old man, and he looked weary and beaten after the service was over. He had reluctantly agreed to stay on in town after the service, but only after Sam had agreed to ride out to the mine with him the next day.

The door opened and Margaret walked into the room. She smiled brightly on seeing Sam, his chest bared, sitting up in bed. 'If you hadn't promised to go out to the mine with Harry this morning, I'd make you pay for that blatantly seductive pose you are striking there,' she warned light-heartedly.

Sam quickly pulled up the sheets to his chin and gave her an offended look. 'I really don't know what you mean by that,' he proclaimed innocently. 'You walk into a man's bedroom unannounced, and then threaten him with physical violence just because he has a bare chest.'

The girl's face registered an impish grin, and she hurried across the room to grab the edge of the sheet and pulled hard. Sam held on to the upper edge with a firm grasp, and he laughed loudly.

'I'll scream rape,' he threatened.

'It's a bit late for that,' she replied, as she changed her point of attack, sliding her hand up under the edge of the sheet. This move caught Sam by surprise, and she nearly made her target before his hand clamped down to trap her wrist with his fingers.

'That's a low shot,' he chuckled, before bending forward and kissing her lightly on the lips. 'I'm tempted to return the threat – but Harry will be waiting for me.'

Margaret stopped her attack, and Sam released his grip on her wrist so she could sit back. 'Can I come out to the mine with you?' she asked hopefully. 'I hate the thought of being stuck here all day by myself.'

Sam thought about her request for a moment. He could see no reason why she couldn't accompany them out to the mine – especially since Sheriff Mandall had convinced him that now the Wooley brothers were dead there would be no more trouble.

'Yes, you can come out with us,' Sam confirmed, and quickly received a hug and kiss from the girl as payment.

'That's enough for now, Margaret,' he declared, breaking away from her when her kiss started to become too demanding. 'You had better let me get up and get dressed. Harry will be sitting down there waiting for me.'

'He is,' the girl informed him glumly. 'Tom Mandall is also down in the kitchen waiting to talk to you. He said he was thinking of riding out to see Jim Carlton and Igor Vlahov, and that he was hoping to ride part of the way with you and Harry.'

Sam climbed out of the bed and attempted to get dressed. He still had to avoid the girl's grasping hands, but he succeeded in keeping clear of her long enough to get fully clothed. He then reached out to pick up his personal possessions that were lying on the bedside table, and put them in his pockets. The last item he picked up was a silver half-hunter pocket watch, and he gently wound its mechanism.

'That's a beautiful watch,' Margaret observed. 'What a shame it's been damaged.'

A dent showed clearly in the case, and Sam looked down at the timepiece in his hand. His thoughts had turned back to the frail young girl who had given it to him many years before, and he felt a flush of warmth as her image came into his mind. She had given him the watch just before he had ridden out to hunt down her father's killers, and he had carried it ever since. Sam had been no more than a kid of seventeen years of age at the time, but he still vividly remembered how close he had come to death when the watch had deflected a killer's bullet right in front of his heart. The watch, along with the promise he had made at the girl's grave-side, stood as a constant reminder that he must always use his skill with a sixgun to defend those who were less able to defend themselves.

Returning his thoughts to the present, Sam turned and headed for the door. 'Let's go downstairs,' he proposed, but had only taken a few steps when he heard a yelp from behind as Margaret jumped on to his back and wrapped her arms around his neck. She laughed loudly as he fought to break her grasp, but when this failed he walked backwards and collapsed back on top of her on the bed. They wrestled on the bed for several seconds before Sam finally managed to turn around in her grasp and look down into her happy, laughing face. She had a wild streak about her that he found exciting, but he also found that he really enjoyed her company. She was a deep person who kept her emotions well hidden, and Sam realized that he liked her very much.

'Come on, let's go downstairs,' he declared, and then gave her one last kiss before climbing back to his feet and helping her off the bed.

As they were walking from the room she took hold of his arm and stopped him. 'I love you, Sam,' she confessed, and on seeing the frown that instantly formed on his brow she continued, 'I don't want you to say anything. I just wanted you to know – that's all.'

The girl then walked from the room leaving Sam to follow quietly along behind her, but her words still rang in his ears. He didn't love Margaret, but he realized that given time he might well come to do so.

They found Tom Mandall and Harry Bird sitting at the kitchen-table drinking coffee, and the look on the old miner's face showed he wasn't in a good mood.

'About damn time too,' he growled. 'You think I got nothing better to do than to sit down here twiddling my thumbs while you play games up in that bedroom?'

Sam felt a flush of embarrassment colour his face as he realized that the noise of his wrestle with the girl on the bed must have carried down to the two older men in the kitchen. He knew that he had done nothing to be ashamed of, but he still felt uncomfortable at the thought that he had been enjoying himself in the house of the two people who had so recently died.

'I'm sorry, Harry,' he apologized. 'I guess I've been a bit insensitive.'

'A bit!' Harry scoffed, but Tom Mandall quickly jumped to the young couple's defence.

'You're an old sourpuss, Harry,' he declared. 'You're only jealous that they are having fun and you're not. We're all sad that Elizabeth and George are dead, but it doesn't mean that everyone has to walk around as though it's the end of the world, and are not allowed to smile or laugh. You and George were partners for quite a few years, and if you don't know that he would have wanted these youngsters to get on with their lives and to enjoy themselves – then you knew very little about him.'

It was now Harry Bird's turn to be embarrassed, and he sat speechless for some time before he finally cleared his throat and spoke. 'Maybe you're right, Tom. I'm sorry if I've upset you two – but I guess I'm just a bit grouchy at the moment.'

This was the first time that Sam had heard him apologize about anything. It had even sounded sincere, but he decided that to discuss the subject further would benefit no one so he instead chose to change the subject to Tom Mandall's trip to the Golden Spirit Mine.

'Why are you going out to see Igor Vlahov, Tom?' he asked as he sat down at the table. 'Do you now think he was involved with Mike Wooley and his men?'

'Actually, I'm more interested in having a talk to Jim Carlton,' he replied. 'I've already spoken to him about his involvement with the Wooley brothers, but there are still a few things I want to clear up with him before I can drop the matter.'

Margaret placed a plate of hot food on the table in front of Sam, and she was about to sit down beside him when her attention was drawn by the sound of the bell from the shop.

'I think I have a customer,' she explained, as she headed across the room towards the doorway that led out into the shop.

Sam forked some hot pancake into his mouth and was chewing on it when he suddenly remembered the threat he had heard the mine foreman make to George Martin the day he had walked in on them in the store. Quickly swallowing the food in his mouth, he told the town sheriff about what he had heard that day.

'It sounds as if he was talking about you, Sam,' Harry Bird opined before the sheriff could speak.

'You could be right there, Harry,' Tom Mandall conceded. 'The more I think about this whole situation, the more I'm starting to suspect Jim Carlton. I remember Igor Vlahov once telling me that both Carlton and the Wooley brothers had arrived together at his mine looking for work. It was just after that shipment of gold from the Golden Spirit Mine was hijacked, and they had arrived offering to protect any future shipments – and since their arrival there has been no further trouble.'

'Surely that is suspicious in itself,' Sam declared. 'I know the Wooley brothers were pretty good with their side-arms, but it seems strange to me that no one has tried to hijack the gold shipment again since they arrived. Did you ever catch the outlaws who carried it out?'

'No,' the sheriff answered. 'The hold-up happened just the other side of the county border, and that put it outside my jurisdiction. As yet I haven't heard all that much about it, except that it was carried out by four men on horseback, and that they got away with ten thousand dollars in gold. I also know that they made sure that no one could identify them by killing the driver and the two guards.'

Sam found his interest in food had suddenly disappeared and he pushed his plate aside. It sickened him to think that innocent people should die just because they were doing their jobs – but he didn't kid himself that any man desperate enough to steal another man's gold would have a conscience about killing innocent people. 'Where did Jim Carlton and the Wooley brothers come from?' he enquired.

Tom Mandall frowned as he considered this question, and he didn't sound too sure when he answered. 'I think they came from Los Angeles. They rode into town around eight months back, and headed straight out to the Golden Spirit Mine.'

'Don't you find that suspicious?' Sam asked. 'How long was it after the hijacking?'

Once again the sheriff thought hard, but it was Harry Bird who spoke out. 'It was about two weeks after the hold-up. I remember it clearly because George and me had to come into town to meet Elizabeth and Margaret who had just arrived on the stagecoach. We were standing out the front on the street when they rode in.'

Further conversation on this subject was forestalled when Margaret re-entered the room with James Morgan. She walked across and sat down at the table next to Sam, and left Morgan standing in the doorway looking uncomfortable.

'What can we do for you, James?' Tom Mandall enquired.

'I've come over here to talk to Harry,' the president of the Local Business Association replied hesitantly. 'But I'd like to speak to him in private.'

'Anything you've got to say to me can be said right here in front of everyone,' Harry Bird growled stubbornly, and the visitor showed his discomfort at this by breaking out into a sheen of perspiration on his brow.

Morgan looked to be unnerved by this

directive from the old miner, and he hesitated before finally speaking. 'I was wondering whether you might reconsider selling your mine to Igor Vlahov now that you've lost your partner and will be forced to work it by yourself?'

Harry Bird's reply was explosive and he stood up so quickly that he nearly knocked the table over. He then lunged for James Morgan with his arms outstretched, but Sam was between them and was able to block his path.

'I'll kill you with my bare hands you low life scum!' Harry shouted, but Sam was able to hold him by the shirt until Tom Mandall could move around the table to help pull him well clear of Morgan.

'Calm down, Harry!' Sam cautioned, but the old man was far from regaining control of his temper. He continued to struggle in the grasp of his two companions as he tried to reach James Morgan.

'Get out of here, Morgan,' Tom Mandall instructed, as the man stood back against the wall, a stunned look on his face. 'George Martin isn't even cold in his grave yet, and you come in here talking about money. If you don't get moving right now I'll let Harry loose, and I'll swear that he killed you in self-defence when he goes to court for your murder.'

James Morgan quickly turned on his heels and left the room, leaving behind him a deathly silence until the bell on the front door of the shop was heard. Harry Bird then gave out an explosive sigh, and his companions released their grip on him.

'Are you all right, Harry?' Sam asked.

'That man turns my stomach,' he stated angrily as he attempted to straighten his clothing. 'If he comes near me again I'll wring his damn neck with my bare hands.'

Sam looked across to Margaret and saw that she had tears in her eyes. She was breathing deeply to control her emotions, and he realised instantly that this confrontation had done little to help her get over the deaths of her mother and uncle.

'Are you all right?' he asked, as he walked across and put his arms around her – and she nodded her head in reply.

'I'm really looking forward to my day out at the mine with you,' she informed him, hesitantly.

'We should take a picnic lunch with us and have it on the river bank,' Sam suggested, and Margaret raised her head and smiled up at him lovingly. The other two men realized what Sam was doing, and joined in to talk about anything but the deaths of her mother and uncle, while the girl set about preparing the picnic hamper.

FIFTEEN

The wagon rattled along with Sam holding the reins. Margaret Martin was sitting on the seat beside him, and the further away from town they got the happier she seemed to become. Sam guessed that getting away from the town for the day was giving her a break from the things that continually reminded her of her mother and uncle, and that this was just the medicine she needed at this present time. He knew it was going to take her some time to fully recover from their deaths, and knew also that he wanted very much to help her do so.

Sheriff Tom Mandall and Harry Bird were riding along in front of the wagon, maintaining an easy pace as they closed in on the turn-off to the mine. They were still about half a mile short of the turn-off when they suddenly reined in, forcing Sam to follow suit so as not to run into the back of them. A couple of riders were waiting on their horses in the middle of the road up in front of them, making no attempt to move their mounts on seeing their approach.

Sam recognized the two riders as Igor Vlahov and Jim Carlton. An uneasy feeling settled over him as he eyed the pair so he dropped his hand to the sixgun at his side and eased the weapon from its holster. He felt there was going to be trouble, and this was confirmed when he saw that Igor Vlahov's hands were tied together in front of him, and that Jim Carlton was holding a gun aimed at the mine owner's back.

'I think it would be a good idea if you *hombres* dropped your weapons,' Jim Carlton demanded. 'And make it quick or I'll blow Vlahov's brains out.'

There was no immediate response from Sam and his companions and Carlton cocked the hammer of his gun to emphasize his demand.

'You must think we're damned stupid, Carlton,' Harry Bird accused. 'If you think we're going to fall for the old trick of holding a gun to the head of one of your own men in an attempt to make us give up our weapons, then you've got a lot to learn. We know Vlahov is behind all this and you can't kid us otherwise.'

'You're a stupid old fool,' Carlton snapped in reply. 'You and Vlahov make a good pair.

You've spent half your lives digging around in holes under the ground, and you've lost your grip on reality. The reality of this situation is that my men will shoot you out of the saddle if you don't drop your guns right now – and the girl will get it first.'

Sam quickly looked off to his left and right, and saw that there were mounted gunmen in the cover of the bushes on both sides of the road, and that they had their rifles trained on both him and Margaret.

'Drop your gun, Harry,' he quickly instructed the old miner. 'They've got us surrounded, and they look serious about shooting Margaret.'

Both Harry and Tom looked around and saw the two gunmen in the bushes, and they quickly dropped their weapons and raised their hands in the air.

'You won't get away with this, Jim,' Tom Mandall warned. 'All you are doing is proving that the rumours are true that you were in with the Wooley brothers.'

'They are true,' the mine foreman chuckled. 'But that knowledge will be of little help once I've finished with you.'

'Please don't do anything to harm them, Jim,' Margaret Martin begged, but this plea fell on deaf ears.

'I suggest that you stay out of this, Margaret,' Carlton threatened. 'Or you will die with them.'

This threat angered Sam, but there was little he could do about it. With the risk that Margaret could be injured if they tried to put up a fight, they had little choice but to go along with Carlton's instructions, and wait for a chance to fight back when there was less risk to the girl.

'We'd better do as he wants,' he advised his companions as he too threw down his weapon.

The gunman on Sam's left climbed down from his horse and walked across to pick up the weapons. He also collected Harry's and Tom's rifles from their saddle-boots, and then took Sam's rifle from the back of the wagon.

Jim Carlton waited until the gunman had returned to his mount before speaking out again. 'You three get up on to the back of the wagon,' he instructed Igor, Tom and Harry. 'And if any of you make a false move I'll kill you.'

Once Igor, Tom and Harry had settled down into the back of the wagon behind Sam and Margaret, the mine foreman once again gave out instructions. 'Start the wagon moving now, Brady, and just remember, the girl gets the first bullet if you try anything.'

This threat made Sam think hard. He had been trying to come up with a plan that would give them a good chance of escaping while at the same time minimizing the risk of injury to his companions. The best he had come up with so far was to wait until they were on the move again, then push the team into a full stretched gallop and try to break away from Carlton and his men – but this plan was quickly discarded because it presented too much of a risk for himself and his companions, especially now that they were unarmed. Instead he started the horses at an easy pace, and Carlton and his men fell in behind the wagon with their weapons drawn and ready for use.

It seemed to take only minutes before the turn-off came into view, and Sam was surprised when Jim Carlton directed him to take the turn-off towards Harry's mine, and not to continue straight on towards the Golden Spirit Mine.

There had been no talk between Sam and his companions since the ambush, and even Margaret was quiet and withdrawn. She had said nothing since begging Carlton to let them go, and Sam realized that the foreman's threat must have really shaken her.

Sam began to feel panic rise inside him as he knew that time was quickly running out. He would have gladly taken the risk of trying to escape if he was by himself, but in this situation he couldn't bring himself to risk the lives of his companions in the wagon. He was at least grateful that Carlton had hinted that he was going to spare Margaret's life, but this was cold comfort for the three men in the back of the wagon.

The sun was directly overhead as they made their way along the valley floor towards the canyon mouth, and the valley was bathed in sunlight. Sam glanced around to see that Carlton and his men were still in close company with their weapons drawn, and they were as wary as ever.

'What do you think they're going to do with us, Tom?' Sam heard Harry Bird ask from behind him.

'I wouldn't have a clue,' the sheriff replied solemnly.

Igor Vlahov then spoke out. 'Carlton said he was going to give us a funeral that would become part of the local folklore, and when I asked him what he meant by it he refused to answer. He did say, though, that he was doing it because he was sick of having nothing while people like me and Harry have everything, and that we don't even value it.'

'That's a damn fool thing to say,' Harry growled in return. 'I've worked hard for everything I've got, and I never had it given to me on a silver platter like some I could name.'

'Well that couldn't include me then, Harry,' Igor declared. 'My parents spent their lives scraping together enough money to send me to college so I could study for a degree in geology. They both died from cholera before I could repay them, but I can assure you that I earned every cent I have with these two hands.'

'You studied geology?' Harry asked, and a new look came over his face as he eyed the Russian with interest.

'Sure did,' Igor answered.

'Shut your yap!' Jim Carlton shouted from where he was riding behind the wagon, and the three men promptly obeyed.

Sam pushed this from his mind as he forced himself to concentrate on the situation at hand. He had to concede that their predicament seemed hopeless, and that he had little choice but to wait for an opportunity to present itself for him to try something. The ride from there on in to Harry Bird's mine was done in silence, each man wondering what their fate was to be. Margaret looked across at Sam only once, and his heart sank when he saw that tears were flowing freely. He gave her a smile that was aimed at giving her strength, but she just shook her head defeatedly and turned her head away.

'Stop the wagon in front of the cabin,' Carlton directed as they closed in on the mine workings.

Two men walked out of the cabin and stood in the open waiting for them to approach. As Sam pulled the wagon to a halt in front of them, Jim Carlton moved forward to speak to them. 'No problems?' he asked.

'No, there was no one here when we arrived,' one of the men replied.

'It's not too late to give yourself up, Carlton,' Sam said. 'I'm sure the judge would take it into consideration at your trial.'

This brought a mocking laugh from Jim Carlton that was echoed by the men accompanying him. 'You must think I'm stupid, Brady. I hold all the cards in this game, and I'm also going to win the pot. But you and me have a little score to settle first.'

'What little score?' Sam asked warily.

'Later,' was Carlton's abrupt reply, and he turned away to organize his men. 'Kurt, take the girl into the cabin and keep an eye on her – and make sure she stays there.'

One of the men quickly dismounted and moved across to help her down from the wagon. She walked off towards the cabin with the gunman, but on reaching the cabin door she hesitated. She looked back at Sam and seemed to be about to say something, but her eyes moved across to Jim Carlton and instead she dropped her gaze and walked into the cabin.

Sam understood what she was going through. She would be deeply concerned about the fate of her four companions on the wagon, but the threat that Carlton had made earlier had served to make her fear for her life. Sam was grateful that Carlton seemed intent on sparing the girl's life, but wondered how he intended keeping her from telling all once she was free of him.

'Move the wagon over to the mine entrance,' Carlton instructed Sam, and the young ranger did as he was bid.

Once the wagon had stopped Sam and his companions were instructed to climb down to the ground. They were then lined up and Jim Carlton and the remaining three gunmen stood facing them with their sixguns drawn.

'You three move over and stand just inside the mine,' Carlton instructed the three older men. 'Jack, you keep them covered – and if any of them try anything kill them all.'

Carlton then waited until his instruction had been carried out before he turned his attention back to Sam. 'The last time we met you made a fool of me in front of everyone,' he accused. 'You may have won that time but this time I'm going to have the pleasure of beating you to a pulp, and you won't be able to do anything about it.'

Carlton then reholstered his weapon and moved towards Sam with his fists raised. Sam instinctively raised his hands in readiness to defend himself, but Carlton stopped and smiled. 'No, Mr Brady. You don't fight back, you just stand and take it – and if you raise one hand in your own defence I'll kill the girl.'

Sam's face drained of colour. He felt like killing this man with his bare hands, but knew that if he wanted Margaret to have a chance of surviving this situation, he would have to do as Jim Carlton was demanding. He dropped his hands down to his sides, and then waited for Carlton to make his move.

It wasn't long in coming, and the mine foreman stepped forward and sank his fist into Sam's stomach. A second punch caught him in an uppercut under the chin, and the young ranger's head snapped back and he fell to the ground gasping for air.

'Come on, get up,' Carlton demanded as he sank his boot into Sam's ribs.

'Let him alone, Carlton, you yellow-bellied coyote,' Harry Bird remonstrated, but this only served to make Carlton more determined, and he struck out again with his boot.

This time Sam managed to roll clear of the blow and he climbed groggily to his feet – but Carlton was already moving in again. He landed two more solid blows to the younger man's head, and he then stood back to watch Sam fall to the ground, stunned.

Another kick landed in Sam's ribs, and he knew he was now beyond defending himself. He braced himself for a beating, but the sound of Margaret's near-hysterical voice penetrated his agony.

'No, Jim,' she cried. 'If you want me to co-operate with you, you mustn't hurt him any more.'

Sam lay where he had fallen, expecting any

moment to feel the boot once again landing against his ribs – but when nothing happened he opened his eyes to see Carlton standing over him breathing heavily. Margaret Martin stood some twenty feet away behind him with tears running down her face, and the foreman seemed to be considering her demands.

Suddenly, Carlton turned and confronted her. 'All right – but get back to the cabin right now and don't show your face again, or I'll shoot you myself.'

Margaret turned and started walking back towards the cabin, and the gunman Jim Carlton had earlier detailed to guard the girl started back with her.

'Next time I give you a job, Kurt, I expect you to carry it out,' Carlton shouted after him. 'And if you ever let me down again I'll kill you.'

The gunman's step faltered at this threat directed at him, but then he grabbed the girl by the arm and hurried her back towards the cabin.

Carlton turned back around to face Sam. 'You'd be dead by now if she hadn't intervened, Brady, but don't go getting your hopes up because you're going to die even more slowly now.' He turned his attention to

162

one of his men. 'Mick, take the bullets out of their weapons and pile them up a good distance back in the tunnel – and then come back out here.'

The gunman did as instructed, and quickly disappeared from view into the tunnel. Carlton stood watching Sam while they waited for the gunman's return. He had a twinkle of amusement in his eyes, and finally Sam could hold his tongue no longer.

'What are you going to do with us, Carlton?' he asked.

'You just wait and see,' was his sneering reply.

The gunman returned after several minutes, and Carlton instantly barked another command. 'Tom and Harry, come over here and help your injured friend. I then want you all to go down inside the tunnel, and if you're quick enough you might be able to get your weapons and reload them before we get too much of a head start on you.'

Igor Vlahov led the way in through the mine entrance, and Harry and Tom followed along behind half carrying Sam between them. As the tunnel closed around them, Tom Mandall spoke. 'What do you think he's up to, Sam?'

'I don't know,' was the younger man's

reply. 'But as soon as we are out of their sight let go of me and I'll make a dash for my gun – and with a bit of luck I'll be able to get back outside and get a shot at them before they can get out of range.'

The two older men nodded their agreement, and the plan was given a boost when they found a lighted lantern just inside the entrance. Sam looked back over his shoulder and saw they were some thirty feet into the tunnel, and he reached out and took the lighted lantern from Igor Vlahov before making his move. He broke free of the other two men, and ignoring the pain in his ribs started off along the tunnel at a jog. The pain was breathtaking, but his mind was focused on finding the pile of weapons he was looking for. The weapons soon came into view, and he dropped to his knees beside them and tugged his sixgun from its holster. He quickly fed shells into its chambers, and then climbed back to his feet and headed back towards the entrance. He found the three older men slowly making their way along the tunnel, and he handed the lantern to Tom Mandall as he passed by.

'The guns are about fifty feet back along there,' he informed them. 'As soon as you're armed, come back out to the entrance.'

'Be careful,' Tom Mandall warned, but Sam was already moving towards the entrance in a shuffling run. He slowed when the opening of the tunnel came into view, and then moved over to the side and hugged the wall for cover as he cautiously moved forward. He was still some twenty feet from the entrance when there was a deafening roar and the roof of the tunnel began to fall in on him.

SIXTEEN

The deafening roar of the falling rock and dirt finally abated, and Sam dragged himself back up on to his feet. It was now so dark inside the tunnel that he couldn't even see his hand in front of his face. He could feel pain in his left shoulder where a falling rock had hit him, and when he explored the area with his fingers he could feel the stickiness of blood soaking his shirt. After further examination he realized that it was only a graze, so he turned his mind to the situation that he and the other three men now found themselves in. The rock-fall at the entrance of the tunnel had entombed them behind hundreds of tons of rock and dirt, and to attempt to dig themselves out would be a long and energy-sapping task. A feeling of claustrophobia threatened to overwhelm him, but he managed to subdue this by turning his mind to the other three men trapped in the mine with him.

'Are you OK back there?' he shouted into the darkness.

'Yes, but you stay where you are until I can find the lamp and light it again,' Harry Bird instructed him.

Sam did as he was bid and after several minutes he saw the faint glow of a light further back in the tunnel. It seemed like an eternity before he could finally make out the shapes of the three men moving towards him, and a feeling of relief settled over him on seeing that they were unhurt.

'We thought you might've been buried under a rock-fall, young fella,' Igor Vlahov admitted. 'I'm glad to see you weren't.'

'Thanks Igor,' Sam smiled, as he moved back to where the other three men were standing. 'But I might as well have been buried, because it's going to take us a lifetime to dig ourselves out of here.'

'It'd take more than a bunch of coyotes like Carlton and his men to beat me,' Harry Bird growled. 'And you're a damn fool for thinking they have, Sam.'

'Well, seeing that Carlton has blown half the hillside down over the only entrance, I think I've got good cause to think we're beaten.'

'Do you two agree with him?' Harry asked of Tom Mandall and Igor Vlahov.

'It does seem pretty grim,' the sheriff

opined, and Igor Vlahov nodded his agreement.

'Ye of so little faith,' Harry scoffed before turning and limping away towards the depths of the mine.

'Where the hell are you going with that lamp?' Sam asked in exasperation. 'We're going to need it out here if we have any chance of digging ourselves out.'

The old miner stopped and looked back. 'If we dig ourselves out, Jim Carlton and his men will be out there waiting to put us straight back in here and bury us again – or shoot us. So, why don't you put your trust in me and just follow?'

'What the hell are you up to, Harry?' Tom Mandall asked, and the tone of his voice showed he was in no mood to put up with further antics from the old man.

'All right, I'll explain,' Harry relented grudgingly. 'There's another way out of here.'

'Then why the hell didn't you tell us that in the first place?' Tom Mandall asked irritably, but Harry ignored this question and instead started off along the tunnel once again. The three men followed along behind him in silence, but more than once they were heard to mutter oaths as they stumbled over rubble on the floor of the tunnel.

'How much further is this second entrance?' Sam enquired testily after some time.

'We're nearly there,' was all he got back in reply, but it was another five minutes before they finally stopped.

'Here we are,' Harry advised his three companions, but they were puzzled by what they saw. They had come to the end of a branch tunnel, and all they could see was a pile of rocks and dirt that seemed as impenetrable as that which blocked the front entrance of the mine.

'Where's the entrance, Harry?' Igor Vlahov asked for all three of them. 'I didn't want to say anything before, but by my reckoning I'd say we're somewhere in the middle of the hill between your valley and mine.'

A smile lit the old miner's face as he answered. 'You're exactly right – we are. Some time back George and me dug this tunnel and ended up cutting into the end of one of your exploration tunnels. So we filled it in again and made sure that we worked away from this area afterwards.'

Sam sighed with relief. He had begun to think that Harry had gone mad and had led them off into the mine to die, but now he understood what he was up to. He saw a couple of shovels and a wheelbarrow lying back against the pile of dirt, and moved forward to pick up one of the implements. 'Where do I dig?' he asked.

'Right where you're standing,' Harry directed as he picked up the second shovel and passed it to Tom Mandall. 'I left the shovels and wheelbarrow down here just in case we ever had a cave-in, and luckily we've never had to use them up until now.'

'How much dirt is there to move?' Sam enquired.

Harry took hold of the wheelbarrow and moved it back so they would have room to work before he answered. 'It'd take one man about half a day to move it all – so on my reckoning it should take us a couple of hours.'

'Why the hell did you put so much dirt back in here?' Tom Mandall asked, voicing Sam's thoughts.

'Since George left, I found it easier sometimes to dump some dirt back in here rather than cart it all the way out to the entrance,' he confessed guiltily, and no more was said on the subject as they organized themselves into moving the overburden out of the way.

Sam and Tom started shovelling the dirt and rocks into the wheelbarrow, and they then rested while Harry moved the waste back along the tunnel and dumped it. Igor soon stepped forward to take the shovel from Sam, who was still suffering from the effect of the beating that Jim Carlton had given him. The four men then took it in turns to dig away at the overburden and to push the wheelbarrow, but after two hours they seemed no closer to making a break-through than they had when they had first started.

'Are you sure that this tunnel joins up with Igor's tunnel?' Tom Mandall asked breath-lessly, when he stepped back from the rock to take a rest.

Harry was too exhausted to speak, and merely nodded his head determinedly in reply – but he began to think that he might have moved a lot more overburden into the tunnel than he had first thought.

Sam returned to the tunnel with the empty wheelbarrow and he leaned back wearily against the wall and rested while his companions set about refilling it. His face was covered in a sheen of perspiration, and his body ached from head to toe, but what distressed him most was that his breathing was becoming more ragged. Suddenly he realized that this was due to the reducing levels of oxygen in the tunnel, and that if the tunnel turned out to be a dead end they would all end up slowly suffocating to death.

It was another hour before anyone spoke again, and this time it was Harry Bird who expressed his concern. 'Maybe your men back-filled the tunnel at your end, Igor?' he croaked tiredly. 'We should have hit it by now if it was still open.'

Harry's three companions looked at each other through the flickering light given off by the lantern, but no one bothered to answer him. This was their only hope of survival, and they would either live or die right here.

Sam took the shovel from Harry Bird's hands and began to shovel again. His body was numb to the pain now, and his clothes were plastered to his body from the perspiration that soaked them, but the thought of what Carlton might be doing to Margaret drove him on.

The three older men realized what was motivating the young man, and they silently settled in to help him once again. It was around twenty minutes later that a section of the roof near the top of the face fell in, and a hole large enough for a man to crawl through suddenly appeared before them. All four men cheered wildly as they scrambled up through the hole into the other tunnel, and the dirt that plastered their sweat-soaked clothing and faces didn't even seem to bother them.

'We need a plan for when we get out the other side,' Sam insisted as they started along the tunnel towards freedom. 'We're going to need a posse large enough to take on Carlton and his men – and we're lucky to have our sidearms back but we'll also need some rifles.'

'I've got some rifles at my cabin,' Igor Vlahov assured them. 'We can even use some of my miners as a posse to save the time we'd waste by having to go into town to get one.'

Sam couldn't see the Russian's face as they moved along the tunnel but he knew that he was waiting for his next question. 'Can you trust the men at the mine?'

A dry chuckle escaped the Russian. 'I might have made a big mistake in choosing a mine foreman, but I can assure you that the rest of my men are reasonably honest and law-abiding.'

'We can only hope you're right,' Harry Bird muttered.

The four men found the going much easier now, and the tunnel was wide enough for them to walk two abreast. As the entrance to the tunnel came into view, the mine owner called them to a halt.

'We keep an armed guard on the entrance to the mine,' he advised. 'I'll have to warn him that we're coming out.'

'What if he's one of Carlton's men?' Tom Mandall asked.

'Then we're in big trouble,' Vlahov grinned. 'But I'm sure it will be OK. Carlton would have taken all his men with him over to Harry's mine.'

Igor Vlahov moved forward and halted just inside the entrance. 'Jack Jones, can you hear me?' he shouted.

'Who's in there?' the guard demanded quickly.

'It's Igor Vlahov,' he informed him. 'I'm coming out with my hands in the air – so don't shoot.'

Igor disappeared from view. The three men left inside the tunnel could hear muted voices from outside, but they couldn't hear what was being said. After several minutes, the Russian reappeared accompanied by a second man who was carrying a rifle in his hands.

'You're having a joke on me,' the man declared on seeing the other three men standing inside the mine. 'You hid in there before I came on shift, and you're just playing a joke, surely?'

'It's the truth, Jack,' Igor assured him. 'But we don't have time now to prove it to you, we've got more pressing matters to attend to. I want you to go over and rouse the men, and get them over to my cabin so I can tell them what's happening.'

The guard turned to leave, but Sam called him to stop. 'Could you leave me your rifle?' he requested. The response from the guard was hesitant and he looked at his employer for guidance.

'Do as he asks, Jack,' Igor instructed. 'I'll guarantee that you will get it back undamaged or I'll replace it with a new one.'

The guard quickly passed the weapon across to Sam. He then turned and ran from the tunnel to carry out his employer's orders.

Sam checked the condition of the rifle and was pleased to find that it was in a clean and serviceable condition. 'I'm going to head for Harry's mine by climbing up over the top of the hill,' he explained. 'When you get the posse organized you can come in through the valley, and hopefully I should have any lookouts taken out by then. I'll have to wait until after nightfall before I can try to get down into the canyon, so give me until one hour after sunset before you ride in.'

'We'll do that, but be careful, Sam,' Tom Mandall warned him.

'I'm coming with you, youngster,' Harry Bird announced to everyone's surprise. 'Them coyotes are going to answer to me for what they did to my mine.'

'No way, Harry,' Sam declared. 'You're too old, and I'll be climbing some pretty steep ground.'

'I can out-work and out-run you any day, you young puppy,' Harry challenged. 'You spend half your life riding around with your arse set firmly in a saddle, and you do very little else. A full day's work in a mine digging ore would kill you – so don't you go telling me I couldn't keep up with you.'

Sam had no answer to this and looked to the other two men for some form of support, but they were both grinning at his discomfort. 'OK, you can come with me,' he finally relented. 'But if you fall behind I'll leave you to fend for yourself– and you had better take this rifle.'

'You'll need that to shoot yourself, Harry,' Tom Mandall quipped with a grin on his face. 'That's what the old Indians do when they get left behind by the young bucks when they're out on the warpath.'

'I'll shoot you,' Harry Bird growled as he grabbed the rifle out of Sam's hand and then started for the mine entrance.

Sam shook his head defeatedly before heading off after him. On exiting the tunnel he found the shadows were lengthening now that the sun was low in the western sky. He hadn't realized that they had spent so long in the tunnels, but now that he thought about it, it had seemed like a lifetime. It was still bright enough to allow Sam to easily pick out the best path to follow Harry, and he hoped that with a bit of luck the light would hold long enough for them to safely cross to the other side. The dangerous part would be descending into the canyon after dark, but he put this concern aside as he forced himself to speed up so as to close the distance on the old miner.

SEVENTEEN

Sam finally caught up to Harry Bird halfway up the side of the hill. His breathing was ragged and short, and his temper was close to the surface.

'For Christ's sake slow down, Harry,' he demanded. 'You'll kill us both before we get there at this rate.'

'Finding the going a bit hard are you, son?' he enquired caustically. 'Maybe you'll learn not to judge people too quickly in the future then.'

Biting back an equally caustic reply, Sam tried to make peace. 'You're right, Harry – and I was wrong. But this is no time to make an issue of something as minor as hurt feelings, especially when we could both die on the other side of this hill if we don't work together.'

The old miner slowed his pace, and allowed Sam to move up next to him. 'You're right, youngster,' he relented. 'But don't ever make the mistake of thinking that I'm too old to be of help. I just want to get over there and help get Margaret out of Jim Carlton's hands before he can hurt her.'

Sam smiled to himself at this confession. He had believed that Harry was only interested in wreaking revenge on Jim Carlton because of the damage that had been done to his mine, but now Sam had to admit that he had been wrong.

'I just don't understand why he didn't put Margaret in the tunnel with us?' Harry pondered aloud.

'I think Carlton had it planned so it would look as if we were all killed in a cave-in, and he probably thought it would look too suspicious for Margaret to be in there with us,' Sam mused. 'But one thing is for sure – he will have to kill her sooner or later to stop her from telling someone about what he did to us.'

There was no further conversation between the two men as they climbed the hillside at a more measured pace. On a couple of occasions they were forced to skirt around some of the larger boulders that scattered the hill, but once they had found the well-defined track that led across the hilltop the going became much easier. It seemed like an eternity to them before they finally reached the crest of the hill, and then started down the incline towards the top of the canyon. They soon reached the spot where the gunman had been firing down on Harry's cabin the day that Sam arrived, and they took cover behind the same rocks and sat viewing the site below.

The sun was now edging down over the western horizon, and the deep shadow that this threw into the canyon below made it look like night. Light could be seen from the open windows of Harry's cabin, and from a campfire burning near the landslide that covered the entrance. Movement near the campfire warned Sam that there were men positioned there to make sure that the men supposedly trapped inside didn't dig themselves out.

'How many men do you see?' Sam asked his old companion.

'What men?' Harry asked as he squinted his eyes in an attempt to see what the younger man was talking about.

'Youngsters do have some uses then, Harry?' Sam asked before he could stop himself.

'So my eyes aren't as good as they used to be,' Harry protested. 'When you spend half your life in dark holes in the ground, you can't expect anything else but to have weakened eyes.'

'I think it's weakened your brain as well,' Sam muttered under his breath, but didn't bother responding to the old man's protest aloud. 'I think I can see two men sitting near the campfire, and maybe another one lying on a bedroll nearby. They will also have a lookout placed at the mouth of the canyon, but it is impossible to see him from here. As soon as the sun has gone I'm going down to take care of him, and then you can come down.'

'I should be the one to go down,' Harry asserted. 'I know that track like the back of my hand, and can make it down there much easier than you.'

'I've got a better job for you, Harry,' Sam assured him. 'I want you to work your way along the hill and then move down behind that group of men near the entrance to the mine. When the posse arrives those men will most likely make a break for it up the canyon, especially after they realize that they are out-numbered, so it will be your job to stop them.'

'I want to help rescue Margaret,' Harry protested.

'I'm not even going to try to rescue her myself until after the sheriff and his posse are inside the canyon,' Sam informed him. 'So if you really want to help her, do as I ask.'

Harry seemed to be about to argue further, but then relented. 'You can be sure they won't get past me,' he contended sullenly, before climbing to his feet and heading off.

Sam watched him go, glad to have him out of his hair while he worked on the next stage of his plan. The last of the sun was now disappearing over the horizon, and Sam looked back over his shoulder and saw that the moon was already high in the eastern sky. He had the choice of waiting until the moonlight was strong enough to light his way down the track to the canyon floor, but he knew this wouldn't leave him enough time to take out the lookout before the posse made its move. Instead he waited a full ten minutes for the gloomy darkness to completely settle in before he moved across to begin his descent.

The track was steep and narrow, and the surface was loose under Sam's feet. He forced himself to concentrate on the track just in front of him, and to forget about the dark void off to his right. At one stage he accidentally dislodged a stone with his foot

183

and it began to roll down the incline, but he managed to stamp his foot down on top of it and stop it. After this incident Sam paused for a moment to settle his nerves, before moving on once more. He was nearly two-thirds of the way down when he heard a noise below him. The moonlight was now bright enough for him to see the shape of a man moving along the canyon floor towards the mouth. Quickly he stopped and drew back into the shadows of the hill and watched the man's progress.

'Hey, Kurt, it's Dave,' the man warned as he approached the bushes at the canyon mouth, and a voice answered him. 'About damn time too – you were supposed to take over from me half an hour ago.'

The rest of the conversation was spoken at a normal level which Sam couldn't hear, but it was only a matter of seconds before one of the men moved off back along the track towards the cabin. Sam could tell by the sound of this man's steps that it wasn't the same man who had identified himself as Dave; the change of lookout had been completed.

The moonlight was getting much brighter, and the rock-face that Sam was descending was now bathed in light. It put him in a precarious position, and he hoped that the men below didn't look up for any reason. He remained in his hiding-place and glanced up at the moon, and was relieved to see that there were several large clouds floating across the sky towards it. It seemed an eternity to him before one of these clouds finally covered the face of the moon and, as the landscape darkened he moved off down the track, making it nearly to the bottom before the moonlight brightened again. After a moment's hesitation he made a dash for the canyon floor and into the cover of some bushes just as the cloud cleared the face of the moon once again.

Sam then settled down and surveyed the area. He couldn't see the lookout positioned at the mouth of the canyon, but he could sense his presence. The lights were still showing brightly from the cabin windows, but there was no one to be seen outside the building, or in its vicinity. The men at the entrance to the mine were blocked from Sam's view by the many bushes that grew along the canyon floor, so he turned his attention back to the lookout. He knew that to try to sneak up on him on this loose rocky ground would be suicide, so he tried to think of a better plan. A ploy that he had been taught by his old partner, Tate Sharp, in his days as a bounty hunter came to mind and he smiled at its simplicity. Tate always claimed that any man who was inside a perimeter defence situation like this was always more alert to approach from the outside, than from the inside in the belief that they were expecting hostility from outside the perimeter and not from within, and thus less alert.

Sam looked up at the sky and watched for the next cloud to approach the moon. His plan was to wait until the moon was once again covered and to then walk straight up to the lookout's position at the canyon's mouth in plain view.

The canyon floor once again darkened and Sam started moving. He walked out of the bushes and turned left along the track. His luck held, because not only was it a large cloud covering the moon but he also saw the lookout light a match and put it to the end of a cigarette. This pinpointed his position and Sam headed straight for him.

Some twenty feet from the lookout's position, the young Texas Ranger was challenged. 'Who's there?'

'It's me,' Sam replied ambiguously. 'Carlton sent me down to take over from you.'

'Is that you, Bob?' the lookout queried.

'Yes,' Sam replied, relieved that he hadn't been asked to identify himself further.

'Why did Carlton send you to take over from me?' the lookout enquired as Sam closed the last few yards. 'I've only just taken over from Kurt, and I wasn't supposed to be relieved for another three hours.'

Sam didn't bother to reply to this question, instead swinging his fist at the lookout's jaw which he targeted by aiming at the cigarette in his mouth. The impact of the punch was diffused when the lookout turned his head at the moment of impact, but the blow was hard enough to stun him and he fell to the ground, moaning. Sam followed up quickly, but this time he used the barrel of his sixgun to strike him across the side of the head. The lookout lay unconscious, unmoving.

Using the belt from the man's trousers, Sam secured his wrists behind his back, and then used his neckerchief to gag him before dragging him into the cover of the bushes.

He then stood and listened for any signs that might indicate that he had been heard by the other men in the canyon, but on hearing nothing unusual he turned his attention to the next stage of his plan. He had forced himself to push thoughts of

Margaret's fate from his mind while he had been trapped in the tunnel, but now that he was in a situation to possibly rescue her, he couldn't help but think that maybe he was too late. He didn't kid himself that he loved the girl, but he found that her love for him and the caring attention she had lavished on him while he was recovering from the injuries he had received in his fight with Carlton, made him want to protect her from any harm.

Another large cloud covered the moon, and Sam took the opportunity to move off along the track towards the cabin. The crunching of the stones under his feet forced him to slow down, but he managed to cover most of the distance to the cabin before the cloud once again began to float clear of the moon. As the canyon floor became bathed in moonlight, Sam took cover behind some bushes and waited. He moved forward again when the next cloud moved in.

On making it to the side of the cabin, Sam could hear voices emanating from inside the building. He recognized the bass rumble of Jim Carlton's voice, and was relieved to hear Margaret's voice answer in return. The words they spoke were unclear, so Sam edged along to the window to see what was happening inside. He saw Jim Carlton sitting at the table drinking from a bottle of whiskey, and seated on the bunk positioned back against the wall was Margaret Martin. Her face looked tired and drawn, and tears welled in her eyes as she watched the mine foreman drinking.

'How long will they last down there?' she asked him.

'Long enough to curse my name, and to regret the day they ever crossed me,' Carlton laughed. 'I'd love to see the face of that pretty boy as he slowly runs out of air. I can't wait until we dig them out again so you can see how he looks.'

'Please dig them out now, Jim. They don't deserve to die like this,' the girl begged, but the response was merely a mocking laugh.

Sam's anger rose inside him, but he forced himself to control it as he moved towards the door. He was pleased to see that Margaret was still alive and well, but he knew that Carlton would get rid of her the moment he thought the men supposedly trapped inside the mine were dead.

This thought forced him to act, and he moved around and knocked on the cabin door. 'It's Bob, Jim,' he reported. 'We can hear them digging, and I thought you should know.'

'Damn them to hell,' Carlton growled as he stomped across the room and yanked open the door, but his face registered shock as he focused on Sam standing in front of him with his sixgun levelled on him.

'Keep your hand clear of your weapon, and back into the room,' Sam instructed, and waited until the man had obeyed before following him inside. He pushed the door closed behind him and took a quick look across at the girl. She was still sitting on the edge of the bunk, and she blinked her eyes in disbelief at seeing Sam. A smile lit her face as their eyes met, but Sam forced himself to concentrate on Jim Carlton.

'Lay your gun on the table, and then back up against the far wall.'

Carlton did as he was bid, and the confused look that played on his face amused Sam.

'You look surprised to see me alive?' he observed.

'How did you get out?'

'We dug a new tunnel right through to the other side of the hill,' Sam replied cryptically, and was even more amused by the disbelieving look that this answer brought to the other man's face.

'I'm so glad to see that you are alive, Sam,' Margaret proclaimed from where she was sitting on the bunk. 'I hated the thought of you dying like that.'

'It's OK, Margaret,' Sam assured her. 'Why don't you get that sixgun off the table and cover Carlton for me while I check on what's happening outside.'

The girl stood up and quickly picked up the weapon. She then levelled it on the mine foreman. Sam opened the door slightly and looked out through the crack for any sign that would indicate that the other men had seen his arrival at the cabin, but all seemed as quiet as before.

Sam closed the door and turned back into the room, but was shocked to find that Jim Carlton had his sixgun back in his hand and it was levelled on him. His own weapon was still in his hand but it was pointed at the floor.

'Drop the gun, Brady,' he instructed. Sam, realising the futility of the situation, did as he was bid. He could see Margaret standing beside Carlton, and she looked sadly across at him.

'I'm sorry, Sam,' she declared. 'But it was either you or me – and I'm afraid you miss out.'

'Why, Margaret?' Sam enquired. 'Are you mixed up in all this?'

'I suppose you could say that. You see, Jim Carlton is my husband. We've been working together for some time now at getting this mine, and as a bonus we look like getting Golden Spirit Mine as well. You were an enjoyable interlude Sam, but you are in our way now.'

Sam couldn't believe his ears. He shook his head as if hoping that it was all a dream, but the stark reality of the sixgun muzzle pointing at him told him it was real. 'You killed your uncle and mother just so you could get this mine?'

'We were only planning on killing George, but Mother forced us to kill her as well. She was helping us with the plan to make Harry and George sell out, but when we told her we were going to kill them both she threatened to tell the sheriff what we were up to.'

'So what are you going to do now?' Sam asked.

'Kill you,' the girl replied casually. 'And then we'll have to go and find the other three who escaped with you and finish them off as well.'

The sound of many horses riding into the

canyon could be heard and the look on Jim Carlton's face showed that he knew it meant trouble.

'It sounds as if you are a bit too late,' Sam informed them both. 'That's the sheriff with his posse, and you'd be doing yourself a big favour by giving up right now.'

'We will hang just the same whether we've killed two or three people,' Jim Carlton growled and lifted his sixgun at arm's length and took aim on Sam, but just as he was about to pull the trigger Margaret struck out and knocked his arm aside. The bullet missed Sam's head by inches, and the gunman cursed savagely and swung out his free hand striking the girl in the face. She fell to the floor, but Sam didn't have time to worry about her because he was already diving across the room to knock the candle from the table. The candle went out as it hit the floor and the room was thrown into darkness. Jim Carlton didn't wait around and he ran for the cabin door. On reaching the doorway he fired several shots back into the darkened room, and then disappeared out into the night.

Sam crawled back across the floor to retrieve his sixgun, and found it lying where he had dropped it moments earlier. Shots could now be heard outside in the darkness, and warily he edged towards the door intent on following the foreman, but the sound of moaning coming from the back of the room stopped him short, and he turned back into the room.

'Are you all right, Margaret?' he asked, but on receiving no reply from the girl he reholstered his sixgun and moved across to retrieve the candle. Setting it back in its holder, he put a lighted match to its still smouldering wick. The girl lay on the floor against the wall showing no signs of movement.

Sam hurried across and knelt down beside her, and then took her up into his arms. He carried her across and laid her on the bunk. She seemed to be unconscious, and Sam thought that she might have hit her head after being struck by Carlton, but then saw blood soaking the front of her blouse and a thin trickle running from the corner of her mouth. Sam felt totally powerless as he wiped this blood away with his neckerchief. Her breathing was very ragged, and fluid could be heard rattling in her lungs with each laboured breath.

She had been hit by one of the bullets that her husband had fired back into the room as he ran from the cabin. She had saved Sam's life by knocking Carlton's arm aside and Sam wondered why she had done it as she had only just told him that they were going to kill him – but, he guessed, she couldn't carry it through at the last moment.

Margaret coughed harshly, and then opened her eyes. She looked up into Sam's face, and a sad smile settled on her lips. 'I'm sorry, Sam,' she apologized, and a tear ran from the corner of her eye.

'It's OK, Margaret,' he comforted her, knowing that she was very close to death. 'I forgive you.'

'I really do love you,' she confessed, in a rasping whisper, and then gave a final breath that sounded like a sigh before relaxing back on the bed as if falling into a deep sleep – but she was dead.

Sam squeezed her hand in his own and leant forward and kissed her before walking from the cabin. Once outside, he met up with Igor Vlahov and some of the possemen who had the cabin surrounded. Quickly he told them that Carlton had escaped, so they moved off to help Tom Mandall and his men who were involved in a gun battle with the men near the tunnel.

Sam was intent on finding Jim Carlton. There was no sign of him in the area around the cabin and Sam knew that Carlton would try to put as much distance as possible between himself and the posse. Carlton's first aim would be to get himself a horse, and then some food to take with him on the trail, and the quickest and easiest way for him to get these would be to climb the track and make for the Golden Spirit Mine.

Sam looked up at the hillside and surveyed the track that was illuminated in the moonlight. He thought he saw a shadow moving about halfway up and then heard a stone rolling noisily down the rock-face. The young Texas Ranger broke into a run for the base of the track, all the while wishing that he had a rifle that he could use to pick Carlton off, but he knew that every minute he wasted before getting after Carlton would increase the gunman's chance of making good his escape.

Sam scrambled up the steep canyon wall as fast as he could, rocks and gravel rolling away noisily behind him, but this didn't register on his mind as he focused on the pursuit of the fugitive in front of him. Sam caught a fleeting glance of Carlton up in front of him as he edged around a narrow section of the track, and he snapped off a quick shot at him.

'You damn idiot,' he castigated himself as he realized he had wasted a shot by shooting at Carlton over such an impossible range. He then set his mind on closing the distance on his quarry, and swore to himself that he would not fire his weapon again until he had Carlton squarely in his sights. The steepness of the track began to ease away, and although Sam's breathing was strained and coming in short gasps, he forced himself on even faster.

The buzz of the bullet as it sang past his head was the first thing that Sam heard, quickly followed by the sound of a handgun being fired. Throwing himself to the ground, Sam surveyed the area in front of him, but he couldn't see any movement amongst the dark shadows that were thrown by the larger rocks up on the hilltop. He wondered if Jim Carlton was still there, so he decided to find out. He knew he was still outside accurate range of a handgun, so he climbed to his feet and moved forward once again. A second bullet buzzed close by him, but this time the muzzle flash from the mine foreman's sixgun gave away his position. Sam once again hugged the ground and then started forward on his hands and knees, determined that nothing was going to stop him from capturing Jim Carlton.

The crack of a rifle being fired up on the hillside stopped Sam, and he wondered where it had come from. He lay there listening to the sounds coming from below at the mining camp, but there was nothing to be heard up in front of him. Where the hell did that rifle fire come from? he asked himself, and this question was soon answered.

'Sam – this is Harry,' a voice announced. 'I've shot and killed Jim Carlton.'

'Damn it,' was all Sam said as he climbed to his feet and walked wearily up the hillside. Harry Bird was sitting on a rock beside the sprawled figure of Carlton, a toothy smile on the old man's face.

'I got the varmint,' he declared. 'I moved in behind him and told him to drop his gun, but he decided instead to try to out-shoot me.'

'You did a good job, Harry,' Sam congratulated him, but he couldn't help but feel cheated by the older man's intrusion in the gunfight.

'Us oldies are at least useful for something then?' Harry asserted, continuing the argument he and Sam had been having earlier. 'You may even learn something from me if you hang around long enough.'

A sudden thought struck Sam and he eyed the older man with a raised eyebrow. 'How come you're still up here on this hill? I thought you were going to work your way down into the canyon behind Carlton's men and stop them from escaping that way.'

'You've always got to pick fault,' Harry growled sullenly. 'All right, I admit that I couldn't climb down there because my legs were too tired – are you happy now?'

'Happy and relieved,' Sam admitted, as he patted the old man on the shoulder good-humouredly. 'If you hadn't killed Jim Carlton, I would've probably got myself killed trying to take him – so, thanks.'

They left the body where it lay and began working their way back down the track towards the canyon floor, Sam helping the older man when it was too steep for him to manage by himself.

EIGHTEEN

Tom Mandall pulled his horse to a halt outside the front of Harry Bird's cabin. He climbed down off his mount and went inside where he found Sam, Harry, and Igor sitting around the table. He smiled warmly and shook hands with each of them before sitting down.

'I'm really sad that you haven't changed your mind about leaving, Sam,' he stated. 'Are you sure you won't stay on as my deputy?'

'I appreciate the offer Tom, and I'm sorry to have to turn you down,' the young ranger proclaimed. 'I'm keen to get back down into Texas – I think I may even be a bit homesick for it.'

'How can anyone be homesick for that hot, dusty, hell-hole of a place?' Harry Bird scoffed, and this comment brought a chuckle from Igor Vlahov and the sheriff.

'Well, we are going to make you an offer that you surely can't refuse, Sam,' Igor disclosed. 'How would you like to be equal partner with Harry and me in our new mining venture?'

'What new mining venture?' Sam asked.

The two miners grinned widely, and Igor went on to explain. 'We've decided to join our two mining operations together and make one big mine. We're going to open up that tunnel that joins the two mines together, and then run the ore through the hill to the other side and use my big stamp mill to process it.'

'Congratulations,' Sam offered. 'But I don't see why you should want to offer me a share.'

'You could say you made it all worthwhile,' Harry Bird answered ambiguously. He then pulled a small cotton sack from his pocket and placed it on the table in front of the young ranger. 'Open it, Sam.'

Sam picked up the small sack, surprised by its weight. He tentatively untied the pull-string and eased the top of the sack open. The contents glistened brightly in the light, and Sam could feel his throat constrict as he viewed the gold that filled the small sack.

'Wow,' was all he could say, bringing laughter from the other three men.

'It has that effect on me too,' Igor informed him. 'And there is a lot more where that came from.'

'But why do you want me to be a partner?' Sam asked again. 'You two own your mines and are just combining them into a single operation – I've got absolutely nothing to contribute.'

Igor Vlahov's gold teeth glistened as he smiled. 'As Harry has already said, you are responsible for this gold in a way. You see, if you hadn't stirred up Jim Carlton the way you did, and forced him to try to get rid of us by burying us in Harry's mine, we might never have found the richest vein of gold I have ever seen in all my years as a miner.'

Sam frowned deeply and shook his head confusedly. He didn't have a clue what these men were talking about, and he was about to say so when Harry interjected.

'It's not all that difficult to work out, youngster,' he taunted. 'When Carlton's men blew the canyon wall down to block the tunnel they uncovered a rich vein of gold. You see, we've been mining this hill thinking the gold was to be found at ground level, but now we know the richest veins are higher up on the hillside. This mine might even turn out to be one of the richest gold deposits in California, and we're offering you a share in it.'

Sam thought about the offer and was pleased that the two miners had bothered to consider including him. He still couldn't understand why they were offering it to him, and his face must have showed his indecision.

'Don't go taxing your brain by thinking too hard,' Harry Bird demanded. 'Let's just say us miners believe in always standing by our partners, and without hesitation you risked your life for a grumpy old fool like me. So the least I could do is offer you George Martin's share of the mine in return for everything you've done for me.'

This confession from the old miner embarrassed Sam and he sat speechless. 'I really don't know what to say,' he finally replied.

'"Yes" would do to start with,' Tom Mandall chuckled.

'No,' Sam answered. 'I mean, it's very generous of you to offer me this, but I just can't picture myself down there under that hill breaking rock. I love being on the trail and sleeping under the stars – I know it sounds corny, but that's me.'

'We thought you might say that,' Igor Vlahov admitted, and placed a piece of paper on the table in front of the younger man. 'We've already given Tom one of these, so you can have this to take with you.'

'What is it?' Sam asked as he pulled the sheet of paper closer so he could read it.

'It's ten thousand dollars deposited in the bank in your name,' Harry informed him. 'We guessed you might turn us down, so this is our way of saying thank you, and if you ever need our help just contact us and we'll be there for you.'

Realizing that it would be stupid to turn down this gift, Sam placed the slip in his shirt pocket before shaking hands with the two as a way of saying thank you. 'I'm glad that everything has turned out OK, and I promise you that I'll never forget my trip to California as long as I live.'

The four men finished their drinks and moved outside to where Sam's mount was tied. As he was climbing up into the saddle, Harry spoke out again. 'We've decided to give our new mine the name "Brady's Cache" – what do you think of that, Sam?'

A broad grin lit the young ranger's face and he shook his head bemusedly. 'You really know how to embarrass a man, Harry,' he declared before wishing his new friends goodbye. The three older men then watched the youngster turn his horse and start it off along the trail that led out of the canyon. They saw him look across towards the track that led up the canyon wall as he passed by it, but had no idea what was in his mind at that moment.

Sam's thoughts had returned to the gun battle fought here in the canyon four days earlier. Jim Carlton and Margaret Martin had been the only ones to die that day, although one of the possemen and a couple of Carlton's men had been slightly wounded. Jim Carlton had been buried the next day in an unmarked section of the town cemetery, and the girl had been buried next to her mother and uncle. Sam hadn't told anyone what Margaret had told him that night in the cabin, and he intended that it would remain his secret. He now believed Margaret was the one who had shot the gunman in the alleyway the day of the gunfight with Mike Wooley, and had thus saved his life – but now he would never be able to prove it. Margaret Martin had been a person who had wanted the best from life without having to work for it, but her love for Sam had cost her her own life, and in so doing he hoped that she had found her way into heaven.

The publishers hope that this book has given you enjoyable reading. Large Print Books are especially designed to be as easy to see and hold as possible. If you wish a complete list of our books please ask at your local library or write directly to:

Dales Large Print Books
Magna House, Long Preston,
Skipton, North Yorkshire.
BD23 4ND

This Large Print Book, for people
who cannot read normal print,
is published under the auspices of

THE ULVERSCROFT FOUNDATION